The picture of them kissing was one of the first to come up.

Words like *mystery woman*, *future king* and *hideout* popped out at her. But that didn't matter when other words were more pressing. Like her name. Her town. Her store. They mentioned May, but not by name, which was the only source of relief she had from the entire thing.

If she had done this search before all of this had happened, she wouldn't be in the papers or on the internet. May wouldn't be a daughter, four years of age, father unknown.

She regretted giving Kade privacy. She probably shouldn't have—her intentions had been noble—but what did noble matter when her daughter was in danger?

Damn it.

Her heart cracked, emotion all about spilling out of it. But she couldn't give in. She'd have to put on her rain boots, take out her umbrella and maneuver through it.

Dear Reader,

It always brings me a special kind of joy to write royal romances. That should have been enough, but I do love my drama (which, if you read my books, you already know). As such, this book has a twist on the secret-prince trope, a single mother who becomes said prince's boss, and a royal scandal that forces my poor heroine into a world she never could have expected.

Fortunately, she holds her own. It helps that the hero adores her, of course. Since I think we could all use that type of adoration in our lives, please enjoy Prince Kade's complete and utter devotion to you. Oops—I meant to his heroine, Amari. ;-)

I hope you'll love them!

Therese

His Princess by Christmas

Therese Beharrie

HARLEQUIN®

Romance™

ISBN-13: 978-1-335-55653-0

His Princess by Christmas

Copyright © 2020 by Therese Beharrie

Harlequin Enterprises ULC
22 Adelaide St. West, 40th Floor
Toronto, Ontario M5H 4E3, Canada
www.Harlequin.com

Printed in U.S.A.

Being an author has always been **Therese Beharrie**'s dream. But it was only when the corporate world loomed during her final year at university that she realized how soon she wanted that dream to become a reality. So she got serious about her writing and now writes books she wants to see in the world featuring people who look like her for a living. When she's not writing, she's spending time with her husband and dogs in Cape Town, South Africa. She admits that this is a perfect life and is grateful for it.

Books by Therese Beharrie

Harlequin Romance

Billionaires for Heiresses

Second Chance with Her Billionaire
From Heiress to Mom

Conveniently Wed, Royally Bound

United by Their Royal Baby
Falling for His Convenient Queen

Tempted by the Billionaire Next Door
Surprise Baby, Second Chance
Her Festive Flirtation
Island Fling with the Tycoon
Her Twin Baby Secret
Marrying His Runaway Heiress

Visit the Author Profile page at Harlequin.com.

To the princes in my life.

I love you all more than I thought possible.

CHAPTER ONE

WHEN THE BELL attached to the door of her store rang, Amari Hayes didn't immediately look up. She had some things to do before she officially opened. But being in a small town meant people didn't pay attention to the rules very well. She had learnt that during the three and a half years she'd been a resident of Swell Valley.

She'd also learnt it was fine for her to make her own rules. She finished what she was doing, *then* she looked up. And stared.

And stared, and stared, and stared.

He was tall. Tall enough that she had to lift her chin to make eye contact, which rarely happened since she herself was tall. That would have been enough to snag her attention, but he was also quite deliciously built. Strong and thick; the kind of body that could easily swoop her into his arms during an emergency.

He was impeccably dressed in a tailored suit. Blue. The suit was blue. Normally, the colour of a suit wouldn't matter. But *this* blue on *this* man was something special. It matched his brown skin perfectly and did something for his dark features. Heavy-set brows, the polite pull of his angular cheekbones, his lush mouth.

It was ridiculous to make such superficial observations about a man, let alone feel a rush of…something, in her body as a result. He was a stranger. He deserved respect, not lust.

It was interesting, that was all. She hadn't had a feeling like this since…since her husband. Her *ex*-husband.

She cleared her throat. 'Hi.'

'Hello.'

She got nothing else.

'The store isn't officially open yet,' she said, trying not to shift her weight. 'If you wait another five minutes—' She broke off. He clearly wasn't from Swell Valley, and it was pointless making him wait five minutes so she could, what? Get herself a cup of coffee? 'What can I help you with?'

'I'd like to speak with the manager.'

'You already are.'

'Oh.' Surprise coloured his expression. 'You're the manager?'

'I'm the owner. But those roles are interchangeable around here.' She tilted her head. 'Did you expect someone else?'

His polite expression returned, but a light blush tinted the skin of his cheeks.

'It was rude of me to show surprise,' he said evenly. 'I'm sorry.'

'For showing surprise, or for feeling it?'

'Both.'

She studied him again, but this time it had nothing to do with his appearance. It was that practised lilt of his voice. His measured tone that didn't waver, even when he was surprised or embarrassed. The politeness that seemed to spill from his pores.

They didn't get many people like this in Swell Valley. The town was a stone's throw away from Cape Town, its population about ten thousand, and everyone knew one another. That meant an authenticity that wasn't practised, measured or polite.

When Amari had first moved to Swell Valley, that level of comfort had bothered her. People had asked her about May, her daughter, as if May were their own. They would enquire about her well-being, about how she was getting on at day-care, about whether she'd overcome her cold. They would ask Amari if *she* was settling in okay, if she needed help with anything, and when was she going to find a partner to help her with all her responsibilities?

The questions had felt invasive. She came from Cape Town, where people didn't particularly care to ask questions unless they knew her. But the

questions about May…those had put her back up.
She was sensitive when it came to her daughter,
no doubt. Being a single mother did that. Choosing a man who couldn't accept the responsibility
of being a father did that.

But she had moved to Swell Valley to give May
a different life. If she couldn't give her daughter
a family, she would give her a community. Over
the past three and a half years, she had learnt to
accept what came with having a community. She
must have come to expect it, too, if she couldn't
understand this man's demeanour.

'I'm here about the advertisement in the window.'

'What about it?'

'I'd like to apply.'

For the third time in fifteen minutes, Amari
stared. 'You want to apply to be a festive worker?'

The man lifted his chin. 'I would, yes.'

Her eyes travelled down his expensive suit to
his expensive shoes and back up to what would no
doubt be an expensive face had he ever thought
to insure it.

'You realise it's busy work, right? Helping
me stock shelves, assisting customers with their
Christmas shopping.' At his nod, she continued.
'People will come in here and ask your opinion
on what they should get their partners. Or their
in-laws. Or their pets. Are you prepared for that?'

'I'm not sure how to answer that. Am I prepared for the questions? Yes.'

'Are you prepared to *answer*?' This time, she didn't wait for his nod. 'If Mrs Hallow asks what she should get her husband, who works on a farm not far away from here, for Christmas, what would you say?'

He opened his mouth, before closing it with a frown. She shouldn't enjoy it, but it was quite fun to see him emote.

'This store…it sells trinkets?'

Amari looked around, took in the items. To an outsider, they probably did look like trinkets. Along the wall he was closest to there was a glass cabinet with jewellery. Most of it came from locals, as did the crafts that formed the shelf he stood in front of. It was waist high, same as the cabinet, though the shelves behind it, diagonally across the counter where she stood, were higher, and packed with craft materials, knitting material, books, stationery. At the counter, she put the brownies and fudge Mrs Hallow made daily that were delivered by her grandson every morning on his way to work.

Trinkets, she thought again, to someone who didn't understand the workings of a small town. Here, people appreciated being supported by one another. They wanted *to* support one another.

This man wouldn't understand that her business succeeded largely because she carried things locals made and provided things they wanted. He wouldn't know that crafts was one of the most popular activities in Swell Valley, followed closely by knitting, and that many of the items she stocked were a direct result of those activities.

She hadn't expected an outsider to apply for the job. She'd expected a teen on school holiday. But she knew she was late, too. She'd lived in Swell Valley long enough to know that available teens had jobs secured months before Christmas. She had only recently become interested in having a festive helper, or she would have hired someone a long time ago.

If only May had started asking questions about her father in September.

'Sure,' she replied evenly. 'They're trinkets.'

'Then I would ask Mrs Hallow what kind of trinket her husband would like.' He moved forward, stepping right under the air-con. It brought a wave of his cologne towards her. It smelled like power, like control. She shouldn't have liked it. She did. 'If he goes out to the farm, perhaps he'd like…this.'

Amari didn't allow herself the smile. For a second. After that, she couldn't help it.

'A tray?'

'Oh?' He leaned to examine the tray closer. 'I thought it was sun protection of some kind.'

'Sun...' She frowned. 'You're joking, right?'

An emotion she couldn't identify dulled his expression. But a beat later it brightened again, as if someone had flicked a light switch. 'Yes. Yes, of course it was a joke. I know people can't use trays as sun protection.'

Amari bit her lip. Before she could say anything, the door opened.

'We got the Christmas stuff you ordered,' Joe, her delivery man, said by way of greeting. 'Lots of boxes.'

'Oh, I can help,' the man said eagerly.

Amari thought about all the stuff she'd ordered. It was the end of November, and her shelves were barely stocked for Christmas. People would start to do their Christmas shopping soon, and she needed to be ready. And she would need help, too, if she wanted to spend more time with May.

'Do I have a daddy, Mama?'

She closed her eyes against the guilt that still flared days after May had asked the question. It had been innocent, and Amari had known it would come some day. But she still hadn't been prepared. Her solution had been to distract May. She'd given a terribly inadequate answer and had suggested they bake cookies. May had been successfully deterred.

But the more time May spent alone, the more likely she was to think up questions. Unpacking the boxes without help would mean a late night for Amari. May would be sleeping by the time Amari relieved the babysitter and in the morning, May would ask one million questions as was her habit. On the off chance one of those questions was about her father again, Amari needed to find ways to occupy May so it didn't come to that.

It was nowhere near a foolproof plan, but it didn't matter. It made her feel as if she was doing something. Even something stupid, like hire a man who looked like a supermodel to work in her store.

'Fine. You can help me today. We'll use it as a trial period. If it works out, you can have the job.'

She didn't wait for his reaction. Only nodded to Joe to start bringing the boxes in.

Kade didn't know if it was the quaint look of the store or the woman inside it that had made him walk through the door. It was probably neither.

Rather, he'd needed a distraction from the calls that kept coming to his phone. His mother's secretary, the royal communications officer. They knew full well that he was on leave, but that didn't matter when they had the Christmas ball to plan. That was when they would announce the news of his mother's abdication and the date of his coronation. Even walking the quiet streets of Swell Valley couldn't ease the anxiety of all that.

But distraction would.

When he'd had the thought, he'd been right in front of the All and Everything store. His eyes had taken in the advertisement for festive help, then they'd rested on the woman inside. His decision had been made some time after that and he'd walked inside.

He'd put his foot into it when he'd assumed she wasn't the owner, and she'd rightfully called him out for it. His only excuse was that he'd been distracted by her beauty. A pathetic excuse if there was one. His mother would kill him if she knew.

She certainly wouldn't be surprised by the faux pas though. He made them far too often.

Not now.

Yes. He had time before he needed to think about that. Now, he had to deal with his guard, Pete, who he'd managed to convince to hang back when he'd gone inside the store. Of course, Pete had had no idea what Kade intended on doing. When the delivery man had arrived, Pete had appeared in the store, refusing instructions to leave.

'You're under my protection, sir.'

Pete said it in answer to every reason Kade gave as to why Pete should leave him alone.

'Is there a problem?' the owner asked from behind him.

Kade turned. It took him a moment to adjust

to her face, which was what had happened the first time he'd seen her, too. Something about it had his breath catching, though her features were relatively unremarkable separately. The light brown eyes and hair of the same hue. The creases around those eyes, between her brows. Her lips weren't full, nor were they thin; her cheekbones neither sharp nor rounded. But somehow all those features together created something quite remarkable.

Even when they were pulled in disapproval.

'None,' Kade said smoothly. 'This is my guard. He'd like to assist us.'

'Your...guard,' she repeated. 'As in—a bodyguard? Why?' She didn't allow him to answer. 'I mean, you do *look* like a man who would have a bodyguard, but I can't quite marry that with a man who applied for a short-term retail position in a trinket store.'

Kade pretended not to notice Pete's surprise.

'I'll take those questions one by one. First, yes, a bodyguard. It's part of the law of my kingdom that I have protection with me whenever I'm out in public. For this trip, I managed to negotiate one guard only, which I suppose explains his commitment to the job.' Kade sighed. 'As for the rest, you're remarkably astute. The man who needs the bodyguard is not the same man who'd like to help you in your store. The former is a prince; the latter is just a man who'd like to distract himself until he's needed back home.'

He paused, giving her time to process.

'Did I cover all your questions?'

There was a short period of silence. Then she laughed.

At *him*.

CHAPTER TWO

'I'M SORRY.' KADE interrupted the laughter stiffly. 'Did I say something funny?'

'Yes,' she said between giggles. 'You implied you're a prince. Or said it outright, I guess.' She wiped her tears. 'A prince.' She shook her head. 'Wow. Your imagination.'

'I assure you, these are facts, not my imagination.'

The amusement slowly faded from her face. 'You're serious?'

He didn't dignify that question with a verbal answer, only a nod.

'Well, Your Highness, I'm not sure what you're doing in my store. I can't afford to pay royal rates. Or whatever your rate is as an—' she narrowed her eyes '—actor?'

This time he didn't even respond with a nod.

'Okay, I'm not sure what you're looking to accomplish,' she said, serious now. 'I'm the only person who works here. Usually, that's enough. People around here are patient, and that patience extends when they consider you one of their own.' The square of her shoulders told him that was how they considered her. 'Over the holidays though, we get busy. People come from out of town. People in town want nice things. I need help to cater to them, and to get home to my daughter at night at a reasonable time. If this is a joke to you, and you don't intend on helping me, please leave. I'll find someone else.'

It wasn't at all a reasonable response, but Kade's eyes dropped to her hand. She wasn't wearing a ring. Immediately after the observation, he lifted his gaze. He didn't know this woman. Her remarkable face didn't matter. He needed something that would keep his mind busy.

Freedom, he'd realised in the two days he'd spent in the house he was renting, meant time. Time to think, to revisit mistakes, to remember all his mother had done for him and their kingdom. It meant picturing his mother's face when she told him she would be stepping down because her heart condition prevented her from ruling the way the kingdom needed. It meant hearing the plea she didn't have to make verbally: that he not disappoint her.

He needed to focus on that—or *not* focus on it—and not think about the remarkable-looking woman or her marital status.

'This isn't a joke,' he said. 'I'm not an actor. I

am the Crown Prince of Daria, a small kingdom off the shore of Africa. You've never heard of it?'

She shook her head, lips pursed.

'That's fair,' he said, surprising himself with a chuckle. 'We're small, much smaller than even South Africa's landlocked kingdoms of Lesotho or Swaziland. We also tend to keep to ourselves.'

Her lips grew thinner.

'If it would make you feel better, you can—'

Her phone interrupted the suggestion of an Internet search. With one last wary glance at him and Pete, she went to answer.

'Hello, you've reached All and Everything, this is Amari.'

Amari. A remarkable name to suit her face.

As soon as Kade thought it, he shoved it out of his brain. He wouldn't indulge the frisson of attraction. He wouldn't even indulge *thoughts* that leaned in the direction of attraction. He wanted to convince her to hire him. It had become a matter of importance, distraction and pride.

'Is she okay?'

The concern in Amari's voice caught his attention. As did the relieved sigh, followed by a frustrated exhalation.

'Yes. Yes, I can pick her up.'

There were a few more minutes of back and forth before she put down the phone.

'Is everything okay?' he asked.

'My daughter… She had a fall at school. I have to pick her up.' Amari exhaled again, looking at her watch. 'Oh! I have another delivery coming in twenty minutes.' She chewed her lip. 'If I'm not here, they probably won't come again until tomorrow. That means another delay in getting Mr Potter that material he ordered, which would be fine, if he wasn't such a pompous—'

She cut off with a heave of a sigh.

'Amari?' Kade said softly, though he knew she wasn't talking to him. She had merely been talking aloud. 'I can stay here. I can wait for your delivery and help ensure Mr Potter doesn't become irate with you.'

Amari looked at him for a long time. He could all but see the questions in her head. He decided to answer them.

'You have no reason to trust me, but I assure you, I am trustworthy.'

'That's what untrustworthy people say, too,' she said darkly.

'What are your alternatives?' he asked, trying a different tactic. 'You could have your neighbour sign for the delivery? The flower store next door?'

'Sheryl's out for the week after an op. She didn't have time to make arrangements so she closed.'

He didn't know if closing a store due to a medical emergency was the usual way of doing things, or perhaps the usual way of doing things in this town. Either way, if he was lucky, this could work in his favour.

'What about your opposite neighbours? The post office?'

'Monday mornings are their busiest. I don't think they'll have time to sign for a delivery and wait for it to be delivered.'

'It's sounding more and more like I'm your only option.'

Her gaze settled on him. 'I'm taking all the cash with me.'

'Fair.'

'And putting up the closed sign. You won't deal with customers.'

He nodded.

'And if you take anything, just know that… I'll find you.'

His mouth lifted. 'You'll find me?'

'Yeah,' she said, going behind the counter and packing up, including taking the cash in the register. 'You don't blend in very well with your fancy suit.'

He didn't know if that was supposed to be an insult.

'You don't approve of my suit? It has plenty of pockets to steal trinkets. And with the quality of your trinkets, I'm sure they'll go quite well together and no one would be the wiser.'

She opened her mouth, but instead of the fire he expected in response to his sarcasm, he got a huff of laughter. 'Yeah, I get it. You probably don't need my trinkets, huh?' She came around the counter and stopped in front of him. 'Please, *please*, don't make me regret this.'

With a nod for both him and Pete, she left.

They stood in silence for a few moments.

'I'm not sure she should trust us,' Pete said.

'No,' Kade replied. 'But clearly there's some desperation. I understand that.' He gave it a moment. 'Why don't you and I try to find something constructive to do, Pete? Maybe something that won't make her regret her choices.'

Amari had May home and settled within thirty minutes. It was part of the beauty of small-town living. Nothing was far away from anything, and help was easy to find. Like Mrs Green next door, who had eagerly agreed to take care of May for the day while Amari worked.

She had learnt pretty quickly she would have to accept help if she was going to raise May in Swell Valley. Since May only had some bruises from her fall and seemed to be in good spirits, Amari knew this was one of those times. She fussed though, and hoped this incident wouldn't make May ask whether having a daddy would have meant him staying home with her.

Oh, no. She was becoming obsessive. She really needed to get a grip and think about something else. Maybe about how she'd left her store in the care of two men she didn't even know the names of.

She didn't even know their names.

She should have asked. Except knowing their names wouldn't add to their trustworthiness. She had known her ex-husband's name, and he'd let her and their six-month-old daughter down. She had known her mother's name, and the woman had left her to fend for herself for most of her life.

Names didn't mean anything at all.

Get. A. Grip.

She took a deep breath. She had made a choice. A decent one. There was a low probability a man dressed as expensively as that man was—a man who *looked* as expensive as he did—would steal from her store. A man with his imagination would rob a jewellery store, not a bric-à-brac store. And the man who was with him, the man who looked about as dangerous as 'the prince' did expensive... He seemed more capable of crime, yes, but...

What had she done?

By the time she reached the store, she was

a complete mess. She was fully convinced she would return to an empty space but talked herself out of it. It wouldn't be empty; she had only been away for an hour. Half empty, though…

But it was nothing like what she expected when she got there.

The first thing she noticed was her Christmas merchandise. They were packed throughout the store, in no order that she could see, yet somehow still looked festive. Or perhaps the festivity came from the decorations. They'd *decorated*. Two men, one expensive and one dangerous, had put up a ridiculous amount of tinsel on her counters and shelves. Christmas ornaments hung from a small tree set up on the counter. Thankfully, all the ornaments had been confined to that tree.

A Happy Festive Season banner, which was meant to go on sale, not to be used, was currently being pinned to the wall behind the counter.

'Higher, Pete,' the expensive man said to the dangerous man.

Silently, Pete obeyed. Even though he must have known the expensive man was wrong.

'No—not that high.'

Amari watched in amusement as they tried to get the banner straight. It took them an embarrassingly long time, but they managed. Pete noticed her standing there long before Kade did, though he said nothing. She was beginning to like Pete. He seemed like the silent type. Dangerous, but silent.

'Amari,' the man said when he finally noticed she was there. 'You're back.'

The words were a little lame. She pretended not to notice.

'I am. And you've been…busy.'

'Yes.'

He looked around nervously, as if seeing it for the first time. And perhaps he was. Perhaps he was trying to imagine how she was seeing it. A quick glance at his face confirmed her suspicions. He was checking to see how she was responding.

It warmed her. In a weird, totally nonsensical way, this man checking how she was responding to his efforts warmed her.

'It looks great,' she offered, putting him out of his misery. 'I usually don't put up much decorations at the store.'

'You don't?'

Again, the uncertainty had her taking pity on him.

'I leave most of the decorating for home. For my daughter. She's a huge fan of Christmas.'

The man nodded. 'Is she okay?'

'Yeah. She had a fall. Nothing major, but apparently she was crying a lot, and with any head thing they ask parents to keep the child at home for the day.'

'But you're not with her.'

'I have a babysitter with watchful eyes and strict instructions to call if anything goes wrong.' She paused. 'Thanks for asking.'

'Of course.'

There were a few minutes of silence, where the three of them stood and stared at one another. When Amari couldn't take it any more, she walked towards the two men.

'You know my name. It doesn't seem fair that I don't know yours.'

'It's Pr—Kade,' the expensive man said. 'And this is Pete.'

'Nice to meet you both.' She shook their hands. Ignored that little bit of electricity with Kade. It was probably her imagination. 'Thanks for not stealing anything.'

Kade smiled. The electricity that bounced from that smile to her heart wasn't as easy to ignore.

'It was the worst temptation, yet, somehow, we managed.'

She smiled. It was strange, to be caught smiling at him. To have him smiling at her. It felt like a level of familiarity that she shouldn't have with a man she'd only met an hour and a half ago and had spent less than an hour with. She looked away.

'Look…um…about the prince thing…'

'It doesn't have to be an issue if you don't make it one.'

Somehow, the words were gentle. But they made no sense. He wasn't saying that he was joking or lying and yet, those seemed to be the only logical options.

Or no—the one where he was an actor, committed to playing his part, could be an option, too. Or maybe he was simply running away from something.

She understood the desire to run. She had done the same thing when Hank had left. She had been looking for solace and she'd found it in Swell Valley. If people had asked her for more information than she was prepared to give, or poked around in her history, she would likely not have found a home there. But they hadn't. They'd accepted what she was willing to share. Even the half-truths about May's father. If she wanted to give Kade the same courtesy, it would be kind. Fair.

She wanted to be kind and fair. She could handle 'the prince thing' in the name of kindness and fairness.

'Okay.'

'Okay…what?'

'Okay, I won't make this an issue.' She took a moment to get things right in her head, then she said, 'You're hired. Partly because your effort here today is endearing, even if some of it is a little off.' She pointed to a Christmas mug, which had been placed in between knitted scarves. She made a note to ask him about it later. 'And partly because that advertisement has been up for a few days and nobody's responded. If anybody was available in town, they would have already applied.'

'Your confidence in my abilities is overwhelming.'

She liked his dry wit. If he was going to be an employee, that was important. That she liked him. As a person. Not as a man. Not in any way other than as a person who she employed.

'You also proved yourself quite trustworthy today, and, though it was by no means an extensive test, I'll give you a chance. Your probation will be extended to two weeks. I'll pay you a fair wage, starting from today.' She looked at Pete. 'I can pay you for today, too, but I can't have you working here for two weeks. I don't have the budget for you.'

'You don't have to worry about paying either of us,' Kade said, his shoulders oddly stiff.

'Of course I have to pay you. You're working for me. Work means payment.'

'I don't need it.'

She rolled her eyes. 'Everyone needs to feel valued for their work, and, while I can offer you affirmations, money helps, trust me.'

'Amari—'

'I'll pay you in cash, if you don't want to leave a paper trail,' she offered softly. When he didn't reply, she took it as a sign to move on. 'The store opens at eight-thirty. I'll need you here by eight for the latest. On the odd occasion I can't be here to open, you'll need to be here at seven-thirty. Does that work for you?'

'Perfectly.'

'Great.' She put her hands on her hips and looked at the store again. 'Now—care to tell me what you were thinking when you were unpacking this?'

The day went by quickly. Kade was surprised how tired he was when he got back to his rental. It was a two-storey house on a cliff overlooking the beach. Matilda, his secretary, had arranged for the place when she suggested Swell Valley. Apparently, it was where she and her husband stayed when they came to town to visit his family.

He understood why. It was private, the cliff itself forming the edge of the town so it didn't see a lot of traffic. Most of the homes there were owned by foreigners who rented to people like him. This specific one had a comprehensive security system, which was part of why he'd agreed to the suggestion.

The other part was the view.

The décor of the house itself reminded him of the palace in Daria. Dense with its heavy red carpets, gold statues in random shapes, the black furniture. A place that reminded him of home wasn't exactly what he wanted when he was on holiday, but he could set it aside for the sake of that view.

The side of the house that faced the sea—the lounge, entertainment area and dining room—opened up onto balconies. Each balcony had its own table, chairs and greenery. It was more minimal than he expected, but it seemed even the owner understood the main feature was the ocean.

The water was quieter today, the waves lapping against the cliff even though it was almost high tide. The dark blue colour offset the orange sun at the horizon, the orange the only strip between the ocean and the dark blue-grey of sky above it.

Daria was an island; the sea was no stranger to him. Perhaps that was why he felt such a connection to it. He couldn't imagine anything more beautiful, more powerful. He wished—not for the first time—that he could harness that power. How much easier would his role as King be if he could be calm when he needed to be, angry and assertive at other times? And if he could control his emotions as his mother did, would she feel less helpless in letting go of the crown?

He tried his best to do what he thought his mother would approve of, but it never seemed to work. Somehow he always ate more than the polite portion at important dinners, or said something unroyal at important events. He sympathised too much or too little; he wasn't charming enough or he was too charming. All these things he'd heard about himself over the years. All of it from a public he wanted to serve yet could never please.

No wonder his mother was concerned.

If he'd had her instincts, this wouldn't be a problem. But he had his father's.

He had the instincts of a commoner whose kingdom tolerated him because he made their Queen happy.

His parents hadn't been able to have more than one child. His mother had struggled to fall pregnant. By the time they'd discovered they were having him, they had all but given up. At that time, Queen Winifred was already forty years old and high risk, though they were thrilled to have him. And outside the public eye, they were the best parents he could ask for.

But he was certain his parents wished for more than him as a ruler. Surely they didn't want a son the media called 'the Oops Prince' because of his endless mistakes.

The Oops Prince. They called *him*, the future King of Daria, the *Oops Prince*.

Good heavens, it was embarrassing.

It would become more embarrassing once he became King. The Oops King didn't exactly inspire confidence. There had already been whispers about it. Questions about whether he could lead the kingdom when he made mistakes as often as he did.

In truth, it wasn't entirely fair. He might get it wrong on the small things, but he didn't ever cause any political strife.

But then, that didn't sell papers.

At least today, he hadn't felt incompetent. Even when his instincts were off—which they were, often—Amari had asked him about his reasoning, tilted her head in acknowledgement, then explained why it was slightly off. She didn't make him feel bad about it. And through her explanations, he had learnt.

If only it were that easy to learn how to be King.

CHAPTER THREE

'Can I…um…can I help you?' Amari asked after she watched Kade stand in front of the coffee machine for an inordinate amount of time.

He turned around. She sucked in her breath. He had been working for her for two days. Two whole days, and she still hadn't got over how gorgeous he was. She wanted to blame it on the suits, which he still wore, though she repeatedly told him it wasn't necessary. His response had been to compromise; he took his jacket off. And now she got to see how wonderfully a shirt clung to him.

Kind of like she wanted to.

She shook her head.

But it wasn't the suit or the shirt. It was him. There was something about him that…that she shouldn't think about. No. She wasn't there to ponder all the ways Kade's features came together in a rather magnificent work of art. She was there to help him. No—he was there to help her. Right, yes. Help her, in her store.

She swallowed.

'I thought I would get a start on the coffee since it wasn't on when I got here. It's usually on.'

'Yeah,' she said, leaning against the door to the small kitchen at the back of the store. 'Mrs Hallow came earlier than expected to drop off her baked goods today. She came herself since her daughter's taking her to the city.'

'She was here when I arrived.'

'I know.' Because Mrs Hallow had spent a solid portion of the time enquiring about him. Then commenting on how handsome he was. 'But I couldn't take her stuff and send her off. She expects payment.'

'It takes that long to pay her?'

'No.' Amari laughed, and moved into the kitchen when it was clear he still didn't know what he was doing. 'She gets paid when the goods sell, obviously, but she also expects me to talk to her.'

She manoeuvred around Kade, but it felt as if she was very much in his space. Was it because her kitchen was small? Or was it because he took up so much space that *everything* was in his space?

And what was that smell? Power, she'd thought before, but there was more to it now. There was a softness to it. A tenderness. It made no sense and yet somehow it made perfect sense. She gritted her teeth and breathed through her mouth.

'I've noticed that people here like to talk.'

She laughed, and was rewarded for it with another whiff of his smell. Power, softness, tenderness.

Amari.

'Well, it's because you're new,' she said, trying her best to act normal. 'Not only in town—which would have caused some talk anyway, looking the way you do—but because you're working here. For me.'

She filled a jug with water, poured it into the machine, then reached for the coffee. But Kade was standing in front of it, and when he saw her move towards it, he grabbed it and handed it to her.

It was all fairly innocent, if not for the fact that it brought her closer to him than she had ever been. She'd avoided coming close to him before. A combination of self-preservation and the boundaries of an employer/employee relationship. And it had been easy before, too. Pete was usually around, and she would use him as a human shield against Kade. Which worked, since Pete was literally meant to be Kade's shield if she believed their prince/guard story.

She didn't, but whatever. They were helping her. And for the last two days, she'd got home early enough to distract May from any unwanted questions.

But now…now she was caught near his chest, in his gaze. Even without those eyes, liquid brown quicksand she could easily fall into without any hopes of resurfacing, there was his chest. Broad, hard. The kind of chest someone could lay their head on, listen to a heartbeat on, trace patterns on. Someone, of course, that wasn't her. This was all hypothetical, and didn't involve her. She was standing outside the quicksand, her head was nowhere near resting on his chest, and his smell wasn't a hypnotic mist designed to pull her in and never let go.

'Thank you,' she said, shaking her head. She took a deliberate step back, tightening her grip on the coffee.

She praised her fingers for holding steady as she put the coffee in the machine. And then she pressed a button, and let the coffee machine fill the silence vibrating with tension.

It would take a while, so she stepped back, out of the kitchen, and tilted her head. A sign for Kade to follow her. But she didn't ask him to join her because of attraction. No. It was because she wasn't impolite. She couldn't just leave him there, waiting for coffee in an empty room. Never mind that she did it almost every day of her life.

'What did you mean?' Kade asked when they reached the counter.

'What?'

'Inside the kitchen. What did you mean when you said, "looking the way you do"?'

She quirked a brow. 'I didn't peg you as someone who fishes for compliments.'

'Not from everyone,' he said with a small smile. Small or big, that smile was dangerous. More so when he was implying he wanted *her* to compliment him. 'But I admit, it is rather forward of me to ask.' She didn't get a chance to comment. 'What did you mean about you, then? When you said that people would be interested in me because I work for you?'

'They're protective,' she said, booting up her laptop. 'I came to town almost four years ago with a baby in tow and no partner to be seen. People tend to be protective when it comes to babies and single mothers.'

'Single?' he enquired gently.

She looked at him, but there didn't seem to be any hidden motive to his question. He genuinely seemed to want to know.

'May's father…is not in the picture.'

It was an understatement. Hank had taken their picture, torn it up, and used it as confetti as he found another hopelessly in love woman to take advantage of. He'd drawn another picture altogether.

She blew out a small breath, hoping Kade wouldn't notice. But she needed to do something to temper her thoughts, which weren't entirely fair. Hank hadn't woven a spell over her. Her eyes had been open when she married him. No— it wasn't her eyes. It was her heart. But whatever the organ, she had chosen to be with him. She'd adored the way he'd looked at her as if she were the only person in the world. She'd loved his spontaneity that had somehow still felt steeped in reliability. He would take her out of town for a night without warning, but he would pack a bag for her, answer all her questions, be there for her while he did it.

She hadn't been used to it. To the attention, to the *male* attention. Her mother was more concerned with her own life, her own relationships for the most part. Sure, she took care of Amari in the most basic of senses, but she didn't raise her. Amari had to learn emotional cues and support and all the things that should have come from a mother in different ways. One of those ways had been Hank. She was a better mother because of Hank. She only wished May hadn't been collateral damage in her lessons.

'I'm sorry.'

'Don't be,' Amari replied. 'We're better off without him.'

'He wasn't a good person?'

'He was…' She trailed off. 'I don't know how to answer that, Kade.'

He was silent for a moment. 'I think that's answer enough.'

She didn't respond, afraid of what she might say. Not only about Hank—she'd rather not let the bitterness ruin her day—but to Kade. To his startling intuition. To the gentle way he asked questions that never made her feel as if she had to answer, but still made her *want* to answer.

'The coffee should be done now,' she said quietly.

'I'll go get us some cups.'

He left before she could stop him. As if he knew she needed a moment to herself. As if he knew she needed it here, in the store she had built. The legacy she had created for her child.

She took a deep breath and told herself to let it go. The anger at Hank; the gratitude for Kade. Neither would make her a better entrepreneur or mother. And those were her priorities. Her only priorities.

He was rather astounded by the number of things he didn't know. Like the fact that there were different-sized knitting needles, different types of glue, subgenres of romance novels, necklaces that choked a neck rather than hung loosely on a chest. He wasn't sure how much of his ignorance came from being royalty and how much came from being isolated from the interests of normal people.

He had been taught chess, not knitting, because it was strategic and he needed to develop his strategic skills. He'd observed construction works and carpenters, not craftspeople, learning from a distance, only occasionally jumping in, should he some day need to assist in rebuilding his kingdom. He'd read philosophers and sociologists, not romance novels, because those were the approved reading list of a prince.

Being exposed to things he hadn't even known existed now made him feel as if he'd lost out on so much. It made him worry that he didn't have time to learn any of it.

But he did. He had nine more days. He would make the most of it.

'Amari,' he said after they closed the store for the day. Pete had agreed to wait outside. He was guarding the door, but that was as much privacy as Kade would get. 'I was wondering if I could ask you a favour.'

Her eyes flickered up from her laptop. 'If you're going to ask for more brownies, I'm going to start taking it out of your pay.'

'No,' he said, ignoring how his mouth watered at even the idea of brownies. 'Though you should take it out of my pay. That way you won't need to pay me.'

'We're not doing this again.'

They had been since Monday. He understood her frustration.

'No, it was a different favour. I was wondering… Would you teach me how to knit?'

'What?'

'To knit. You know—' He gestured to the knitting material on the shelf.

'Yes, I know. I just… Did you ask me to teach you?'

'Yes.'

'Why?'

'Does it matter?'

'I suppose not,' she said after a minute, 'but it would be nice to know. Some people call it having a conversation, but honestly, what do I know about that?'

He sighed. She got snarky sometimes and, while he appreciated the fire, it did make asking for favours a tad awkward.

'I was never taught. The last few days here have made me think that perhaps it might be worth my while to be taught.'

'Do you want me as your teacher though?'

She offered him a smile. It was knowing, a little self-deprecating, a lot genuine. She knew she wasn't the easiest to please, to talk to, to ask. And yet he still found himself wanting to please her, to talk to her, to ask her things. Because somehow, the fact that it wasn't easy made the smile, the teasing worth more. He knew it defied logic— they'd known one another for three days; surely easy would have been preferable—and yet here he was. Valuing her. Wanting her.

Wanting her.

He'd allowed his mind to go rogue. This is what he got for it. There was no situation where wanting Amari would work. He had to go back to Daria in nine days. He had to take over his mother's crown, deal with the emotions of being a king when the successful previous ruler was still around, then deal with being a son to a woman who had to quit her job because she wasn't well. And that summary was simplifying things.

'Do you know how to knit?' he asked through wooden lips.

Her smile sobered, as if she could sense the change in his mood. She *could* sense the change in his mood. Why else would her own mood change so drastically? It was as if she'd pulled on a cloak of some kind. Disapproval, disappointment were woven into that coat, though the material itself was coolness.

'I know the basics,' she answered.

'I only need to know the basics.'

'Again—are you sure you want me as a teacher? I could ask several other more qualified people.'

'If you're looking for a way to say no, you only have to say the words.'

'I'm not—' She broke off. Her frown deepened. 'I should say no. I don't have the time to teach a man who claims to be a prince how to knit. I have a daughter who needs to believe in the magic of Christmas. I have a daughter,' she said again, more deliberately, 'who needs every second of spare time I have.'

'I understand,' Kade replied, though he didn't. Not completely.

He understood responsibility, of course, more than most. He had an entire kingdom, and, though it was possibly naïve, he thought being responsible for one human child might be equivalent to an entire kingdom.

What he didn't understand was why she was repeating it. Why her tone sounded so adamant, and why she seemed to be reminding herself more than she was talking to him. Did she think she needed the reminder? Had she made some kind of mistake, just as he had, and now she thought she needed to make up for it?

It doesn't matter.

It shouldn't matter, he corrected his thoughts. It shouldn't matter, and yet somehow it did.

Unless he stopped it.

'You're right,' he told her. 'You should spend your time with your family. I'll find someone else to help me. Or I'll help myself. It can't be that hard.'

She opened her mouth, but whatever she was about to say was interrupted by Pete. He flew through the door, slamming it behind him, his back against it.

'What?' Kade asked, alarmed. 'What is it?'

'It's…children.'

Kade rolled his eyes. His bodyguard would save him from a bullet heading his way but heaven forbid that bullet turned into a child. Kade would be dead and he wasn't even sure Pete would mourn him.

'The children's Christmas parade,' Amari offered from behind him. She walked until she was beside Kade and watched Pete with a smile. 'It's a Swell Valley tradition. All the children from the local school participate. They march down Main Road, handing out their letters to Father Christmas on the final day of the school year.'

'But wouldn't that mean they don't believe in Father Christmas? Surely they know they can't hand out their letters to strangers?'

'Ah, but we're not just strangers,' she answered Kade. He noted she'd shifted away from him in the last minutes. 'We're their carrier pigeons. Their postal service.' She narrowed her eyes in thought. 'Come on, take a look.'

'I would rather not,' Pete said, his eyes wide.

'They won't hurt you,' Kade told him.

'So you say,' he replied darkly.

Amari laughed. 'What's your deal with children, Pete?'

It took him a moment, but Pete eventually said, 'Some people get a bite from a dog when they're children and they're scared of dogs for the rest of their lives.'

'Are you saying a child…bit you?'

Now Pete didn't answer, which Amari seemed to take as an answer. She snorted, before looking at Kade. He couldn't help but notice how much more careful her expression had become.

'What about you? Do you have a fear of children?'

'Not at all.'

'Good.'

'Good?'

'You get to see one of our town's best Christmas traditions. Trust me, it's worth it.'

CHAPTER FOUR

SHE REALLY DID think it was worth it. But then, she was biased.

May walked somewhere in the middle of the crowd of children. She preferred not to have attention on her, and she and Amari had agreed the middle was likely the best place for her to be for that.

'But what if you can't see me, Mama?'

It was a real concern. And though Amari had wanted to tell May she would be able to pick her out from the crowd—she was part Amari, after all—she didn't think that would satisfy a four-year-old. Instead, she said, 'Wear your favourite red dress, baby. How can Mama miss you when you're wearing that?'

And that was how Amari came to be staring at a red dress in the middle of the crowd.

'This is great,' Kade said from her side.

Amari stopped herself from jumping just in time. She had forgotten Kade was standing beside her. Or she was trying to forget, since her skin had made gooseflesh its permanent state since they'd come outside.

She was so damn aware of him. Of that broad and strong body, but also of him. His moods. His personality. As if she knew that something had happened when he'd asked her to teach him to knit. She could put it down to her imagination, but she knew that was a lie. Something *had* happened. And she shouldn't care what, but she did.

Focus on your daughter. She needs you.

Yes, May needed her. And she would focus on May. Only on May.

'We do something similar where I'm from,' Kade continued, as if he hadn't made her forget for a second that she wasn't supposed to be indulging thoughts about men she didn't know.

'Where exactly is that now again?'

'Daria,' he answered without a beat. 'It's a small kingdom—'

'I remember.'

'So why did you ask?'

'I was trying to trip you up.'

'I…am not entirely sure I know what that means.'

She turned towards him. 'They don't have colloquial phrases where you're from?'

'Of course they do.' But he was frowning. It was cute. 'I simply…haven't encountered that one.'

'Right. Because you're a prince.'

He sighed. 'I thought we were past this.'

'It's hard to get past royalty.'

'Do you want to hear about our Christmas parade or not?' he asked flatly.

She pursed her lips to hide her smile. He wasn't an easy person to get on the bad side of—it was that damn politeness—but he truly made it worth it.

'Please, tell me.'

He took a deep breath, and when he spoke, it was in his usual measured tone. 'We cordon off the streets of the town and have the oldest families do a procession. People become quite invested. They decorate the stores, the streets, with Christmas decorations. It ends at the palace, where families are invited to offer gifts to the royal family.'

'Your family.'

'Yes.'

She thought about it for a moment. The children's Christmas parade wasn't the only parade they had. It was merely the first, marking the town's official countdown to Christmas. But this one was the most special because it was about the children. Their innocence, their purity, their general excitement for Christmas. It filled the streets much more than the decorations did.

Though lights flickered across the roads, highlighting Christmas reindeers and trees, though almost every storefront was decorated with tinsel and ornaments, though Christmas songs pulsed from large speakers carried by the only float accompanying the parade, it was the children who mattered. The public wanted their letters. They wanted to buy gifts and give them to parents so they'd know what to put under the Christmas tree. They wanted to make Christmas special for the most vulnerable, not the most powerful.

'Are you saying the families of your kingdom bring you and your family gifts?'

'I believe I said that, yes.'

She ignored the dry tone. 'How many families participate in this?'

'I've never counted.'

'Give me an estimate.'

'I'm not sure, Amari. One thousand families? Maybe?'

She blinked. 'Those are a lot of families.' She paused. 'I'm sure those families would benefit more from the royal family providing *them* with gifts, not the other way around.'

May came barrelling towards Amari, preventing Kade from replying. Which was probably a good thing, considering his expression. But soon she had an armful of child and she stopped thinking about it.

'That was real good, baba.'

'Thanks!'

May went on to say a bunch of other stuff and Amari laughed, snuggling her neck and smelling her. She smelled like her baby. Her daughter. She smelled like hope and new life. She smelled like responsibility. May was all those things and more, and Amari was so lucky she could be involved in raising her. And that not only made her angry at Hank, but sad for him. He would never get to experience this.

She had chosen a man who didn't care about experiencing it.

'Amari.'

Amari lowered May to the floor and turned to Kade. 'Sorry. I forgot you were standing there.'

'You had other things on your mind.' He smiled at May, but didn't address her. When he looked at Amari, she realised he was giving her the opportunity to introduce him. He wouldn't do it himself. He wouldn't do it if she didn't want him to. 'I only wanted to say I think it's time for me to leave. Pete's getting anxious.'

For the first time, she realised Pete was standing outside. He had apparently overcome his fear of children to protect his charge. But he stayed on the side, eyes wary. For danger or children, she wasn't sure. Both amused her.

He's so committed to this role.

Just as she was committed to believing it *was* a role.

The alternative was more complicated to consider. If Kade was running from something and needed a bodyguard, he was probably in danger. And that…softened her. Due to a fairly basic level of concern for him, but also because she could relate. For a full year after she left Hank, she had expected him to find her. To demand she come back to him. Or to tell her he wanted May.

There was almost no chance of it happening, but that didn't matter. It wasn't a physical level of danger, but it was the most threatened she had ever felt. She'd even struggled to trust the community around her because of it. What if their concern for her turned into suspicion? What if they looked into her background? What if they hired a private investigator to find out where she came from, what her history was? Fear had made logic irrelevant, so though she knew they probably wouldn't, she still worried.

Perhaps that was why she hadn't looked into Kade's story. There were other factors, of course—looking it up would mean she was indulging someone she was sure was lying; she didn't have time to look up everything people told her that sounded iffy; her gut told her not to—but this was at the core of it. If he was running from something, she would afford him the privacy she'd worried she wouldn't get when she had been running. And because she had got that privacy, and knew how much it meant, she knew he deserved it, too.

'Kade, this is my daughter, May.'

Kade gave May a nod. A nod. As if they were passing one another in the street and were greeting. May giggled, which made Amari smile. It made Kade smile, too.

'It's lovely to meet you, Miss May.'

With another nod, this time at both of them, Kade left.

'He's funny,' May commented after a while.

'He is a bit funny, isn't he?' She stared after Kade for a moment, then pressed a kiss to May's head. 'Why don't we go find something to drink? Maybe we'll get you a cookie, too.'

Kade wasn't prepared for seeing a miniature version of Amari. He wasn't prepared for how it would affect him either.

Protective. It made him feel protective. Little surges of it went through his body the moment he saw that girl in Amari's arms. At first, he couldn't define it. It was a feeling he only had with his parents. And occasionally, with vulnerable people in his kingdom.

But never quite like this.

For all intents and purposes, neither Amari

nor her daughter was vulnerable. Of course, children were inherently vulnerable. But Amari was strong. And fierce. With Amari on her daughter's side, that child wasn't nearly as vulnerable as others. And Amari... She was independent. As he'd said, she was strong and fierce, too. There was no reason to feel protective towards them.

And yet he did.

His response was to stay as far away from her as possible. The last thing he needed was to feel protective towards anyone with the responsibilities he had at home.

'I have to collect some things for the store,' she said on Thursday. 'A lot of things. And my car is in the shop today because the battery has a problem of some kind. So I need to walk. And I'd like another set of hands. Would either you or Pete be interested in helping me?'

Amari's tone was hopeful. So was her expression as she turned to look at both him and Pete. It was faintly alarming.

'I have to go where His Highness goes,' Pete said.

'Well, I actually need someone to stay here.' She gave him a smile that was half smile, half grimace. 'I promise you, it'll only be for twenty minutes. Maybe thirty, if Mr Kyle is in a talkative mode. He's almost never in a talkative mode.'

'Mr Kyle?'

'He makes these candle holders.' She gestured to the shelf. 'He has a batch of new ones for Christmas, and I usually fetch them, which isn't a problem when I have a car. Look, I swear Kade'll be safe. Here or there, he'll be safe.'

'I'm sorry—'

'Pete, please. Please. I can't close the store. It's too busy.' As she said it, another customer came in. No one was at the till yet. 'He'll be safe here. Or with me. With me!' she said as if it just occurred to her. 'Let him come with me. I learnt how to protect myself and May. I can protect him.'

'He's a big man.'

Amari laughed. 'Pete, I can protect him.' A customer came to the counter. 'Please? Also because I've been trying to teach Kade how to use the register for the last four days and it has not been going well.'

Mainly because he was trying to spend as little time with her as possible. Trying to hold his breath. Trying not to feel his skin become more aware or his body pulse. It was a lot harder to focus with all that going on. He had no frame of reference for a cash register and learning it from scratch while holding his breath…

No, it had not been going well at all.

'Amari,' Pete began with a pained look in his

eyes. He was gearing up to say no, but, because he liked her, it was actually bringing him pain.

'Pete,' she said before he could continue. *'Please.'*

They stood looking at one another for a long while. The customer cleared his throat, but neither of them paid attention. Eventually, Pete said, 'Fine. But if you aren't back in twenty minutes—'

'Make it forty. In case Mr Kyle gets chatty.'

'I thought you said thirty?'

'If we're not back in forty minutes, you can come find us.'

'I will.'

'Thank you!'

In a move that was entirely spontaneous, Amari leaned over the counter. It looked as if she was going to kiss Pete. Kade's fingers curled, his body rippling with anger before he could stop it. But she paused.

'I was going to give you a kiss on the cheek, but I realised that might not be welcome.' She lowered to her feet again with a sheepish smile. 'Sorry. That would have been inappropriate.'

'It would have been fine,' Pete said kindly.

The grip of Kade's fist tightened.

'Yes, well, I should ask these things before I do them.' She straightened and looked at the customer. 'I'm sorry, Kent. We'll throw in a free brownie for the wait.'

While Pete helped Kent, Amari gathered her things. She left the address and phone number of Mr Kyle with Pete, as well as her own phone number. It felt strange that they didn't have it yet. They'd seen one another every day for four days and he wouldn't have been able to get in touch with her if he needed to.

It took him a moment to realise strange was actually jealous. He was jealous. Of Pete, and the easiness he shared with Amari. He was jealous that if Pete wanted to, he could pursue Amari. They could have an entirely healthy and happy relationship, even after he went back to Daria.

Pete had that freedom. Kade didn't.

He couldn't be easy around Amari because he was attracted to her. Attraction hadn't done him any good over the years. He was as clumsy about that as he was his royal duties. At times, he wondered if there was something wrong in his brain. Something that made simple, straight-forward things harder. Like the coffee machine. He should have been able to figure out where the water went. Where the coffee went. Why hadn't he?

That might have been a bad example. It was a household appliance that he had no experience with. It was understandable that he struggled. But things like packing shelves? Offering comfort to people in his kingdom? Making a call about what to eat during a cultural visit? Shouldn't those things be easy?

If he led a normal life, if he weren't going to be King, perhaps he would have been able to figure out why his instincts were so off. He might have taken a chance to explore his attraction for Amari, the first attraction he'd felt so fiercely. But he wasn't leading a normal life. He *would* be King. And he couldn't explore feelings, or make choices, or do anything that didn't take his responsibilities into account.

So, yes, he was jealous of Pete.

'You're welcome,' Amari said a few minutes into their walk.

'For what?'

'I freed you from your jailer.'

His lips curved. 'Pete is not my jailer.'

She gave a dramatic sigh. 'It's Stockholm syndrome, isn't it? He's captured you for such a long time, you care about him and feel the need to defend him.'

The smile widened. 'Not quite. He's a little too reluctant to be my type.'

'You have a type?'

'Independent, strong, forthcoming in both traits, and not allowing anyone to get away with anything they shouldn't.'

There was an uncomfortable beat of silence, as if they'd both realised he was describing her.

'Well,' Amari said, giving him a small smile that was slightly tight around the edges, 'I'm sure you'll find that person.'

He thought it best not to reply to that. With his current lack of discretion, he might have said something like, 'I already have'. He would have to pray that the earth opened up and swallowed him then, which might pose a problem for his future reign as King of Daria.

They walked in silence for a bit, Amari leading them through the town paths with the ease of someone who knew where they were going. He took the time to enjoy the town, which he hadn't been able to do since he'd arrived. Then, only a few places had been in the Christmas spirit.

It seemed as if the first week of December was the time the entire town accepted the festive season. Christmas cheer was found on every street, at every corner. Lights flickered on storefronts; Christmas trees shone through windows; wreaths adorned front doors. The bakery on the corner offered them gingerbread biscuits; the convenience store next to them offered small glasses of milk. At the end of the road, two young men stood dressed as elves in front of a gift-wrapping station. They had their phones in their hands, but the moment they saw Amari and Kade, they stuffed both into their pockets and waved.

'Everyone really gets into this, don't they?'

'Yep.'

'What happens if you're not a fan of Christmas?'

She gave him a look out of the corner of her eye, but answered. 'You get used to it.'

'Did you?'

'Oh, yes. May was barely a year old the first time I witnessed the spectacle. I was still so tired, and sad, and… Well, you don't need the details.' Her lips thinned. 'Anyway, I didn't want any part of the festivity. But when the first of December came around, my neighbours started bringing over gingerbread biscuits and mince pies. The day after, I got more substantial dishes. It was like they were using the biscuits and pies as a tester, to check whether I was okay by myself. They were quite invasive, actually.'

'You found that amusing?' he asked, wondering at her.

'Not at the time. At the time, I was spitting angry that these people insisted on coming into my not fully unpacked house with food and cheer. Now though, I realise it was their way.' She shrugged. 'You don't have that at home?'

'No,' he said firmly. 'Where I come from, everyone is very pleased to set boundaries and to respect them. We would never expect anyone to bring us anything, and we certainly wouldn't give anything.'

'It sounds…cold.'

'It can be.' He let it sit for a moment, as that answer didn't entirely feel right. 'We do have a fairly established culture of family though. Extended family, too. So while communities might not be like this, our families are. People take care of their aging parents. If they're faced with tragedy of, say, losing a family member who had a child, that child will be taken care of. It's different from this, certainly, but it's not entirely cold.'

'No,' Amari said, stopping. He stopped with her. 'It doesn't sound cold at all.'

Something danced across her face. It wasn't one of the emotions he had become familiar with the last four days. It was darker than anything he'd seen. If it were a painting, it would be streaks of red and black with barely any glimpses of the canvas.

But there *were* glimpses of the canvas. Small, short, no doubt, but visible. In Amari, it was a vulnerability. It made him step closer to her, as if he could protect her from what she was feeling. Her eyes flickered up to his, rested there. And the red, the black, the darkness, disappeared.

This was a bad idea.

There was no doubt about it. Staring into Kade's eyes, falling into those liquid depths that coated her soul, was a bad idea. That didn't even take into consideration that it felt as if he saw right to her hurt. To her inability to understand the kind of family he was talking about even though it sounded exactly like what she wanted.

Her hand lifted, rested on his chest. She saw it happening. Saw it as if she weren't herself because *she* wasn't doing it. She would never be so forward. She would never let her fingers spread, feeling the ridges of muscles, the strength that she had spent days trying not to think about.

It wasn't her left hand that joined her right, as if it understood the strength of that chest couldn't be held by only one hand.

They were travelling now, down, over his abdomen that was rigid, too, though she didn't know if it was from tension or desire.

She wanted to do more than touch. She wanted to taste. To run her tongue over the plane of his chest, to kiss her way down, over his abs. To trace his muscles. To lick.

She looked up, though she didn't know why. The shock of her desire, of that intensity, should have had her moving away. And yet she was looking at him. In his eyes, which were pools of lust and heat. At the tight lines of his magnificent face, which spoke of a control she should have had over herself.

'I'm sorry,' she whispered, not sure if the apology was for her or for him.

He nodded, accepting it. He covered her hands with his. The heat was as comforting as it was stirring.

Until he moved.

Lowered her hands until they fell between them.

Embarrassed, she tried to pull away, but he tightened his grip.

'Kade,' she said, voice hoarse.

'No,' he replied. 'Don't feel ashamed for what happened.'

'I… I touched you. Without your permission. I… I should be ashamed.'

Gently, he took her chin in his fingers, lifting it so she couldn't keep looking down. So she couldn't keep her shame to herself.

'You had my permission,' he told her. 'I told you with my heart. You must have seen it in my eyes.'

Oh, it was corny. So corny. And yet somehow, she was touched by it. Somehow, she didn't feel it was corny in *her* heart.

'You touched me because we're attracted to one another.'

'No,' she said automatically.

He smiled. 'We'll keep up the pretence, then, shall we?' He nodded. 'You touched me because we're not attracted to one another.'

How he could make her smile in such a torturous moment confused her.

'We can't be attracted to one another.' He wasn't teasing any more. It made sense. This made sense. The tension, the awkwardness. '*I* can't be attracted to you,' he emphasised, letting go of her chin, her hand. 'There is no good that can come from it.'

Of course not. He was running from something. And she…she was running towards something. A life for May that involved stability and reliability. That was all Amari had ever wanted for her daughter. When she'd found out she was pregnant, she had been terrified, but hopeful. That hope came from the determination that her child wouldn't live the life Amari had. Her child wouldn't wonder if her mother cared about her or found her to be a burden. Her child would know that they were loved, unconditionally.

And then Hank had left. Told her he couldn't be a father and left. Amari's dream of giving her daughter more had shattered because she had made a poor choice. She hadn't chosen a good man, a man who could live up to his responsibilities as a husband, a father. Having had a father like that herself—she didn't even know who the man was—Amari had thought herself beyond making that mistake. But Amari had thought herself beyond being like her mother, too.

How was raising a child by herself because of

her choices any different from what her mother had done?

Kade was right. Just as much as he couldn't afford to be attracted to Amari, she couldn't be attracted to him. It would distract her from what she wanted to do: make sure May had the life Amari had always wanted for her. Even if Amari had already let her down.

Because Amari had already let her down.

She cleared her throat. 'You were right the first time. We can't be attracted to one another.'

'Amari—'

'We should…um… We should get those things from Mr Kyle before Pete comes looking for you.'

She started walking before he could reply.

CHAPTER FIVE

'AMARI, DEAR, WILL we be seeing you tonight at the beach?'

Kade heard the question from one of Amari's customers. It slipped past his guard, as had most things since that *moment* they'd shared. He had set up the guard with one purpose: to protect himself from whatever was happening between him and Amari. And he thought it would be easy.

After all, she had set up a guard, too.

From the second he'd told her they couldn't indulge their attraction she'd put distance between them. It had come with tension, and awkwardness, which Pete had merely raised an eyebrow at when they'd returned to the store. His bodyguard didn't mention it when they were alone—he was too professional for that—but Kade often got the eyebrows. He used it as another reminder to wear armour around Amari.

Since then, they communicated for store purposes only. She told him what to do and he did it. When he screwed up, she gently told him how he had and he corrected it. And that was the extent of it.

But things filtered through.

For example, he knew May was having a sleepover tonight. Amari had arranged it the day before. May's friend's mother, who was apparently Amari's friend as well, had come into the store that morning and insisted that Amari grab a bottle of wine from the vintner down the road and enjoy her night. He agreed—Amari had looked particularly exhausted these last few days—but now this woman was asking Amari about going to the beach, and he really wanted to know whether she would be.

'I'm not sure,' Amari was saying.

He tried to pay attention to the customer he was helping. The woman was deciding on whether she wanted the wool that was in stock or whether she wanted to order something from the catalogue. She hadn't made her decision yet. Kade kept listening.

'Lydia has May tonight, doesn't she?'

'Yes, but—'

'Then you should come. We only do the fireworks and wine Christmas evening once a year.'

'But you do a fireworks and wine evening once a month.'

'Those aren't Christmas themed.'

'You mean, you don't wear ridiculous festive attire to those?'

The woman chuckled. 'Exactly. So—I'll see you at seven. I'll keep a seat for you. And—' the woman's voice dropped, though it was quite clear she didn't care who heard her '—bring your two hunky new employees with you.'

'I don't think I'll—'

But a bell rang; the woman had left. At the same time, Kade's customer decided to order from the catalogue. He helped her do so, then went to the front of the store to check for more customers. There were none who wanted help, so he merely looked at Amari.

'You heard that, didn't you?' she asked after a few seconds of silence.

'Yes.'

'I'm so sorry. They've been on about you and Pete for the last week. Wanting to know where you came from and what you were doing here and why I hired you.'

He tensed. He didn't mind Amari knowing the truth, but once more people knew, it would become harder to hide where he was. He had been able to do it until now because his kingdom was small and obscure compared to others. No one cared about a prince from an African kingdom far away. At least, no one here did. But that could easily change. Once people heard the word 'prince' they tended to become more interested. It didn't matter that they hadn't known him before; royalty was the kind of temptation few people could ignore.

His parents had only granted him this leave on the condition that it be kept quiet. It was a short enough trip that they didn't have to make an announcement of any kind. If there were any questions or suspicions about his absence, they would likely be overshadowed by the announcement of his mother's abdication.

Still, he would rather keep his whereabouts private. If the royal reporters knew where he was, he wouldn't have a day of peace. He certainly wouldn't be able to work, and he liked working. He liked the routine of it. He liked feeling useful. More importantly, he liked that it didn't feel as if his mistakes affected thousands of people. He could learn without it being a matter of public interest. He could be corrected without it reflecting poorly on his family, who many believed should have taught him better.

'What did you tell them?' Kade asked.

'That it was none of their business.' She accompanied her answer with a shrewd look, as if to say, *Of course I wouldn't tell them who you are.* 'It doesn't keep them from trying. In fact, I'm sure the only reason they asked me to go was so you two could, too.'

She nodded her head in Pete's direction. He was in the back of the store, fitting a shelf to the back wall. He was proving to be a lot more useful than Kade—unsurprisingly—including suggesting Amari fill the empty space above the kitchen door with a glass shelf that would hold some books.

'I don't think that's true. They probably do want you there.'

'Maybe,' she allowed. 'But it's mostly an excuse for people to get drunk and have fun.'

'I thought it might be. Wine and fireworks at the beach do tend to encourage that assumption.'

'Exactly. And nothing sounds less appealing to me than spending an evening with drunk people.'

'Unless you're drunk, too.'

She dropped her head. 'Excuse me?'

Well, that was a stupid thing to say. Even if Amari hadn't reacted that way, he probably would have thought so. It was presumptuous, for one. He didn't know if she drank, although her friend insisting she get a bottle of wine did seem to be evidence that she did. Still, that didn't account for the fact that he was saying she should get drunk, which was a terrible thing to say to someone. He knew better.

But this was how it was with him. He realised too late that he was saying something stupid. By the time he did, it was out already, and he'd made a fool of himself, regardless of his intentions.

At least he knew he hadn't changed in the last week.

'I only meant that you look like you might need a relaxing evening.'

'I *look* like it?' she asked, leaning on the counter. The casual stance did nothing to take away from the sharpness in her eyes. 'What does that mean exactly? Bags under my eyes? Wrinkles on my forehead?'

'No.' Though the bags part was correct, he had enough common sense to lie. 'I didn't mean it in terms of your appearance.'

'Hmm. I probably shouldn't have assumed that when you said I *look* like I need a relaxing evening.'

He held his tongue. He was going to retort, so he held his tongue.

'Maybe I should have asked instead of assumed,' he said after a moment. 'Do you think you could do with a relaxing evening?'

She narrowed her eyes, then straightened with a sigh. 'I suppose. But I would have had one tonight anyway. In the privacy of my home. With my own wine.'

'And, if I know you well enough, you'd have the store's books cracked open in front of you.'

Her lips parted, but she only ended up frowning, not replying.

'At least at the beach, you'll have people,' he offered gently.

'People are overrated.'

'Perhaps,' he acknowledged. 'But sometimes they offer the kind of distraction you need to feel like yourself again.'

Their gazes held. It felt as if through the contact, they were having a conversation.

She knew he was saying she had offered him some kind of distraction.

He knew she understood. She might have also said that he was offering her distraction, too.

But then she looked away, her guard back in place. He used the time to erect his own shields.

'Consider it,' was all he said, and went to help Pete with the shelf.

She was there because she had a free night. It had nothing to do with Kade.

It was because her daughter was at a sleepover with her best friend and Amari had the night to herself. It was because she would never hear the end of it from Lydia if she didn't do something with her night. That was it. That was the only reason she was at the beach, making small talk, a wine glass in her hand.

Why are you looking for Kade, then?

She ignored the thought. It was getting easier to do, ignoring her thoughts about Kade. The memories were harder. She could still feel his chest beneath her fingers. Could still remember the clenching of his abdomen when she touched him. And the lust. Oh, the lust. She could still feel it wash over her, coating her skin, her breasts, her core. She could still see it in his eyes, in the way he barely breathed, as if inhaling her perfume would break that control he always, always had.

She emptied her glass. When that didn't help, she decided to go for a walk.

The fireworks wouldn't go off until later, when the sky was fully dark and not this mixture of light and navy blue. The sun was already gone, the waves crashing harder against the sand in preparation for high tide. It was a cheat, really, to set an event somewhere near the beach. People saw the beauty of it and immediately thought they'd have a good time. And when people *thought* they'd have a good time, they generally had a good time.

Not her. She had never been one of those 'have a good time' people. She was too serious, too responsible. That was what happened when a child grew up with an irresponsible parent. They assumed the responsibilities of the parent. They assumed the responsibility for *themselves*, which shouldn't happen until they were much older.

Amari could still remember how she would ask her mother to set aside money for her schoolbooks and stationery. She would ask for them months in advance, before the school year even ended, because she knew her mother might not remember. Every month she would remind her mother. And then, when the time drew near, she'd do so weekly, daily. And her mother would usually wait until the very last minute to do so, as if she enjoyed Amari's anxiety.

Even the memory of it now made her faintly nauseous. As did the thought of May ever having to do that with her. She knew everything May needed and made sure she had it. She read every letter May got sent home and signed every form May needed. She checked in with May's teachers regularly.

She didn't want May to be the daughter she had been. Worried about everything. Concerned. Unhappy.

She didn't want to be the mother her mother had been.

But what if I already am?

'Amari?'

She turned at the voice. When she did, she saw the Christmas decorations that flickered in the distance where the gathering was. She hadn't realised she'd walked that far. Which begged the question of why Kade was there.

'What are you doing here?'

'I live here,' Kade said. 'Well, there.' He pointed at a cliff a few metres away.

Amari gaped. 'You live there?' Shook her head. 'Maybe you *are* a prince. Or a millionaire or billionaire because those are the only people who can afford it.' She let it sit for a second. 'Unless you're lying. Did you follow me from the restaurant? Where's Pete?'

'I'm trying to figure out how best to answer you,' Kade said with a small smile when the silence after her questions stretched out longer than she expected. 'I do live there. I came for a walk on the beach, through that path over there.' He pointed. 'It leads to a private beach, which can't be the case if you're here.'

'It's not...' She trailed off. She realised she had come onto the private beach. There were no demarcations apart for some rocks, which she had neatly sidestepped, but everyone knew this property was out of bounds. 'I am, apparently. Although, if they really wanted it to be private, they would have made more of an effort to conceal it.'

'True enough.'

He put his arms behind his back, clasping them. For the first time she noticed how he looked.

Delicious.

He wasn't wearing a suit. Significant, as she had never seen him outside one. More significant were his arms, which he was showing off as though they were cleavage, what with his short-sleeved shirt. It was a dark blue colour, and the sleeves hugged his biceps. Actually *hugged* them, because *clinging* seemed too inadequate to describe just how tight the material around the curves of his muscles was. Dark hair dusted his forearms, which were, unsurprisingly, as defined as the biceps.

Her eyes lowered, taking in the light brown linen trousers he'd paired the shirt with. It was gorgeous against the darker brown of his skin, fitted perfectly, and rolled up at the ankles. He looked like an advertisement for a beach resort, and damn if she didn't want to book an all-inclusive vacation to that resort as soon as she could.

She blinked. Where had that come from? Surely not from her, the person who repeatedly told herself she needed to focus on her kid, on her store. Surely not from the person who had just *reminded* herself of why she needed to focus on her kid and her store.

'As for Pete,' Kade continued, as if there hadn't been a pause after his last words, 'he's around here somewhere. He goes overboard in these spaces.'

'He's afraid someone is going to hide behind one of those rocks?'

'You tease, but I suspect he does.'

Kade gave a smile. A private smile. As if they were sharing some inside joke, or perhaps as if he only gave that smile to her. She wasn't foolish enough to believe that, but she wanted to.

It bothered her. She couldn't trust this attraction. She couldn't trust attraction at all. Attraction had been the first step into the situation with Hank. Then had come the tumble, the fall, hard and fast. She'd lost her bearings; she'd lost herself. She couldn't lose herself with Kade. She had more responsibilities now. More important responsibilities than herself.

'I should… I should get back,' she said, because it was the right thing to do.

'Why did you come out this far?'

'Oh. Um… I was thinking.'

'Thinking?'

'Yes.'

'Would you like to share?'

She huffed out a laugh. 'Only if you want to share why you're here and not living in your kingdom.' She paused. 'Only if you want to share why you came up with a story about being a prince. Only if you want to tell me if you're in danger.'

He frowned. 'I can answer the first question. The rest…' She wasn't sure how it was possible, but the frown deepened. 'You haven't looked me up, have you?'

'I was going to, but every time I wanted to...'

She trailed off. She couldn't tell him she wanted him to have his privacy. He would likely ask why, and the prospect of answering that made her feel oddly vulnerable.

'Well, it made me feel like I was buying into the whole prince story and I'm not,' she settled for. 'It's ridiculous. Princes don't just come to small towns in Africa for a holiday.'

'That's true.' He went silent for a bit, then nodded his head towards his house. 'Would you like to come with me for a drink? Pete will be there, and you'll be perfectly safe. I think it might be easier to explain if we're more...comfortable.'

She shouldn't go. She knew that. Which was obviously why she was nodding and walking with Kade to his house.

The waves crashed at their feet, reminding Amari that the tide was coming in. She didn't move away, instead let the water wet her ankles, her shins. It was summer, the evening was warm, the coolness of the water welcome. She wouldn't be swimming in it any time soon—it was much too icy for that—but the ice was a reprieve from the stickiness on her skin.

Strangely, that stickiness had increased when

CHAPTER SIX

'THROUGH ALL OF this I've never heard the situation described quite so succinctly.'

Kade looked at Amari now. It took him a second to register her reply since, once again, his brain skipped on how good she looked.

She wore a red summer dress that fell to her ankles, a section of which was wet from the waves. It was patterned, with white flowers that had yellow middles, which he didn't care about since the dress plunged at her neckline, giving him a clear look at the swell of her breasts. She had, quite unhelpfully, worn a necklace that dropped just before that swell. It was a simple chain, though the pendant at the bottom was circle of different coloured stones, which he realised matched the dress, including the flowers perfectly.

He noticed because he spent a significant amount of time looking at the pendant and not her cleavage. He would not look at her cleavage.

she'd encountered Kade. Almost as if he had some kind of physical effect on her.

Very strange indeed.

'You're right,' Kade said softly.

'I usually am.' The dry remark had him smiling, as she intended. 'But about what, specifically, this time?'

'Princes don't visit small towns in Africa on holiday.' He didn't give her the chance to reply. 'They do it to regroup. They do it to… Well, I suppose they do it to figure out how they're going to rule a kingdom when they're not quite sure they're made to do so.'

She stopped. 'Hang on—you're telling me you're…what? Going to become King or something?'

It was a little annoying that she was asking when she wasn't entirely sure she believed him. Or maybe it was annoying because she was beginning to believe him.

There were a lot of things about him that were princely. He wore those tailored suits, a new one every day. He didn't know how to do simple things, like work the store's alarm or replace the coffee filter. Then there was the power he carried with him, as if it had been something he was born with. Raised with. Not to mention his accent, which was proper and made her wonder what it would be like to hear him whisper dirty things into her ear.

Focus.

'It's a little of both,' Kade answered. 'I am about to become King, but it's also an "or something" situation. My mother... She's the current monarch. She has been for over forty years. But she has a heart condition, and it's been making her weaker. She no longer feels fit to rule, and she's abdicating.'

'Abdicating? Like giving up the throne?'

'Yes.'

'To you?'

'Yes.'

'Wow.' The word slipped from her lips. It seemed to make Kade's shoulders slump forward, before he straightened them.

'Indeed.'

'That must suck.'

His lashes fluttered. 'Excuse me?'

'It must suck that you're going to become King because your mother's sick. Well, it sucks that your mother's sick at all,' she added, 'but it must especially suck that you now have to do her job because she's sick.'

He turned, looked out at the ocean as he stuffed his hands in his pockets. It seemed like an un-Kade thing to do. It spoke of vulnerability and emotion and it had her stepping forward, taking his hand.

He didn't look at her, or down at their hands. He only held on tight. Something warmed in her chest, but she was sure it wasn't her heart. She had, after Hank, dropped her heart into a bucket of ice and vowed to never defrost it again.

It was unlikely that it would warm now simply because she was holding someone's hand. Kade's hand, sure, but it was still just a hand. He hadn't kissed her, or made love with her, though heaven only knew why she would put either of those options in her head.

Holding someone's hand wasn't worthy of defrosting was all that she was saying. And she was saying it to her heart.

Apparently, it needed the reminder.

Not that it matters. If Amari's noticed, she won't think her pendant is keeping you riveted.

With a shaky breath, he tried to think about the other parts of her. Her hair was loose, the first time he'd seen it as such, the curls of it blowing in the wind. Someone, because he was quite certain it wasn't her, had put a flower in her hair. Her lips were the faintest touch of red, and he wasn't sure if that was because she'd been drinking wine, or because she'd painted them that colour. It mattered to him. He wanted to know whether he would taste wine or simply her if he dipped his head towards her…

'It's my gift.'

He blinked. Her brows knitted, but she clarified.

'Phrasing crappy things in an easily digestible manner.'

'That's a gift?'

'Hmm.' She stayed quiet for a while. 'I suppose that's a valid question. Perhaps it isn't a gift as much as something I taught myself.'

'I… I would like to ask, but I'm not sure whether I'd be pushing if I did.'

Her expression softened. It reminded him that they were still holding hands. It made him feel as if they were the only two people in the world. He knew they weren't. He knew they weren't even the only two people on this beach; Pete was around here somewhere. Yet she made him believe that they were alone. It was…special.

'I appreciate that.' She took a deep breath and looked at the sky. 'My mom…wasn't a queen.' She gave a quick laugh. 'She didn't take a lot of responsibility for me.' She paused. 'It meant that I learnt how to deal with a lot of things myself. She would tell me something…like we were moving, for example. And that was it. No discussion, no reasons. Just the facts. And I had to process it. It helped to talk myself through it, one thing at a time. It helped if I was straightforward and concise about it to myself: *Yes, moving sucks, but you'll still have a roof over your head. Yes, a new school will be hard, but at least no one there will remember you wore the wrong uniform for a month because your mother couldn't be bothered to buy the right one.*'

Her face was tight by the end, her chest moving in and out rapidly. He was about to comfort her when it stopped. All of it just…stopped. She relaxed her face, her lips curving in a self-indulgent manner. Her breathing slowed, the in and out of it deep, careful movements.

And he thought he might be witnessing another side-effect of a negligent mother: self-soothing. Self-control.

It was really quite remarkable, even if it did

leave a dull thud of pain in his chest that she had had to do it.

'It sounds difficult.'

'Not as difficult as ruling a kingdom.'

'Probably as difficult as ruling a kingdom.' He turned, taking her other hand. 'You understand that your experiences are valid in themselves? You don't have to explain them to me, or belittle them because mine seem worse. I swear to you, your pain is as valid as mine. And I'm sorry for it.'

Her eyes widened, her breath *swooshing* through her lips.

'Wow,' she said. 'You really have that Prince Charming thing down, don't you?'

He chuckled lightly. Then it was gone. Gone, because something else took its place. Something intense. Desire, perhaps, though not only physical. There was more to it.

It was that she was strong and independent. He had known it before, but it meant more now knowing that she had made herself that way. She was sharp, her humour dry and pointed, her wit uncompromising and smart. He loved that she was honest about not trusting him, and that her trust was harder to get than anyone else's. She didn't seem fazed that he was a prince. Yes, that might be because she only believed him about fifty per cent, but still. Some people responded in worse ways at the mere possibility.

She pulled him in as if she were a spider and he were caught in her web. Except that analogy only worked if the spider didn't particularly care about catching its prey. Or if the prey had gone willingly into the danger of that web. Because he knew Amari didn't want him. At least not in a way that allowed her to admit it. He knew it just as much as he knew cupping her face between his hands, bringing his forehead to hers was the worst idea he'd had in a long time.

Or perhaps the best.

'My charm would exceed even my own expectations if I got this right,' he whispered, knowing his mouth was centimetres from hers. Knowing, when lust flared in her eyes, that his breath mingling with hers was a temptation.

'This?'

'You know what I mean.'

'I want you to say it.'

'Let me kiss you.'

She answered by giving him exactly what he wanted.

He was only aware of the surface things at first. That her lips were on his, that they were soft, that the red of them had been wine. He felt her face between his hands, heard the faint moan coming from her mouth. The vibration of it slipped through the parting of his lips, accompanied by her tongue. A slight lick, a test, a teasing.

It was all perfectly lovely.

And then he fell beneath the surface.

His mouth opened wider, claiming her as if he were a knight claiming his captured bride. He let her explore, welcomed the hardening of his body, welcomed the softness of hers as she pressed against him. Her tongue was a weapon— no, a tool. When something was used that skilfully, it was a tool. Even if it caused destruction, even if he felt whatever guard he had put up with her be destroyed.

He fell deeper when her hands touched his skin. They lay on his chest first, like the day she had touched him, and they moved down lower as they had on that day, too. His tension this time came not from a clutch for control, but from the acknowledgement that control didn't matter. He didn't care if she touched him, if she felt the way he wanted her. He wanted her to know. He wanted her to touch, to feel, to claim.

But he didn't do it passively. He touched her, too. Lowered his hands to her hips, a plush landing after the sharp features of her face. He let his thumbs stroke her belly, allowed his imagination to linger on what she would feel like beneath the material of her dress. Slowly, his hands went higher. Over the cinch of her waist, stopping at her breasts.

She moaned again, though he only touched the side of her, and suddenly her hands were on his, placing them over her breasts, her nipples pressed into his palms.

'Sir,' came a voice. It took him too long to respond, but he did, removing his hands, shifting so that Amari was behind him.

'What?'

'It's not…private here,' Pete said, his face pained.

He could relate. Kade had never experienced an arousal quite this painful. Pete's pain likely didn't come from the same cause.

'Your timing is ridiculous, Pete.'

'I'm sorry, sir.' He glanced at Amari. 'I'm sorry,' he said again, before turning around. It was as much privacy as he and Amari would get.

Kade angled back to her. 'I'm…sorry, for that.'

She pushed her hair out of her face. It allowed him to see the flush of her skin. An intense disappointment swept over him because he knew if Pete hadn't interrupted, that flush would have been the result of more than just a kiss.

'Hey, it happens.'

'Does it?'

She laughed, breaking the tension. 'Well, I don't usually kiss royalty, but I can imagine.'

She tucked her hair behind her ears. Fascinating, he thought. She toyed with her hair when she was nervous. He hadn't expected that. She was just so…steady, in everything that she did. Nerves didn't seem to fit a woman like that.

But then, Amari did seem to contradict everything he thought he knew about women.

He wasn't complaining.

'I'll… I'll see you at the store tomorrow.'

'You don't want to come for that drink?'

She smiled again. 'I can't imagine what a drink would result in if a walk on the beach did this.' She stepped forward, pressed a kiss to his cheek. 'Tomorrow.'

She greeted Pete and walked away.

He watched her for a long time, then directed his attention to Pete. 'They have a name for people like you, you know.'

Pete sighed. 'It didn't bring me any joy.'

'It didn't bring me any joy either,' Kade said bitterly, and turned to his house.

She was still floating on a cloud when she reached the store the next morning.

Perhaps that was why she fell through it.

'Amari? Amari Hayes?' a man asked.

He had been waiting for her. He was older than her, perhaps in his forties, and there was something about him that was…off.

'Who's asking?'

'Me. Reporter for *Daria Daily*. Is this you?'

He pulled out a picture from his pocket. It was grey, grainy, but it sure as hell was her. She distinctly remembered the moment Kade put his hands on her waist like that. She also remembered where his hands went to next. Where she put them.

'Nope,' she said, taking the picture out of his hand. 'Haven't seen either of those people.'

With a calm she didn't feel, she took out her keys, began opening the door. The man was still talking.

'You don't recognise him? Strange, considering my sources have him working here for the past week.'

She ignored him, and thanked the heavens that the door opened easily. When he made to follow her, she closed the door in his face. Pointedly. Then she locked it. Also pointedly. Then she rushed to turn the alarm off so she wouldn't have the armed response at her door.

That might not have been a bad thing.

Her next move alarmed her. Filled her with shame, too. She *hid*. Hid in the kitchen at the back of the store. Pressed her back into the wall and told herself to breathe. She talked herself off the ledge.

No one could know that was her. No one...

except the people at that party, who had seen her in that dress. But those people were her community. They wouldn't tell a stranger her name, damn it. They wouldn't send them to her store.

But she knew how easily they talked. How they tried to make anyone coming to their little town feel welcome. If someone asked the right questions, made the right noises, she knew they would let information slip.

Oh, yes, that's Amari Hayes. Sweet girl. She owns All and Everything on Main Road. I used to be worried about her, working all alone in that store, but now she has those two gentlemen. Handsome fellows.

Yeah, she could see it. She could see them talking about her, and Kade and Pete, and letting it slip that she was a single mother and that was probably why she needed help from two people instead of one and oh, no! May! They might have told the reporter about May!

If there were noises about her not knowing who the father was, if the reporter made the leap from kissing on the beach to having a child together...

Oh, no...oh, no...oh, no.

She pushed off the wall and headed straight to the phone. Before she could lift it, Kade knocked at the door. His expression was tight, and Pete was nowhere to be seen, and she thought maybe they'd encountered the reporter, too.

She opened it for him, but turned around before he could speak.

'I should have warned you about the man,' she said over her shoulder, 'but I only got here a few minutes ago.'

'Don't apologise.'

Something about the firm way he spoke eased her panic. Still, she dialled Lydia's number with shaky fingers.

'Maybe you should lock the door or something.' She chewed on her nail as the phone rang. It took long. Too long. What if—?

'Hello?'

'Lydia?' Relief nearly choked her. She took a breath. 'Lydia, is everything okay? Is May okay?'

'Everything's fine.' Lydia's voice, which had been faintly dull when she answered, sharpened. 'What's going on?'

'Nothing. Nothing,' she said again. 'Just…you know… I'm not used to May being away from home. Usually, I have her with me in the store on weekends.' She closed her eyes, wondering how much of the lie Lydia would buy.

'Amari, May's fine. They all are. In fact, they're still sleeping.'

'Oh, crap. I forgot. I'm sorry. I forgot the time.'

'Are you sure you're okay?'

She gave a laugh that sounded false even to her own ears. 'Yeah, yeah. I'm fine. Just… They'll have breakfast and you'll take her to school to the make Christmas decorations for the market?'

'That's the plan.'

'Okay.' She exhaled. 'Okay, great. I'll see you then.'

'Amari, you don't sound okay.'

'I'm fine. I'm fine.'

Lydia didn't sound any less concerned by the time she put down the phone, but Amari had done her best. Then she crumpled. Sank into her chair and lay her head on the counter. She allowed herself a minute of it and straightened.

'Sorry,' she said, standing. 'I just had this moment where I imagined them going after her because they think she's connected to you and… I overreacted. I'm sorry you had to witness that.'

Kade hadn't moved from his spot in front of the door. His expression hadn't changed either. Or it had, considering he had come in concerned and now his face held…nothing. It was curiously empty. Practised. She remembered it from that first day he'd walked into her store, asking about the vacancy. She hadn't realised how much he'd relaxed in the past week.

Somehow, the development didn't make her feel any better.

'It wasn't an overreaction.'

She interpreted it as reassurance initially—until the words sank in. 'Wait... Are you telling me that reporter might go after my kid?'

'Not him specifically, no.' Kade took the slightest step forward. 'But those pictures of us are splashed across every newspaper in my kingdom at the moment.' He gestured to the picture she still held in her hand. She'd forgotten about it. 'They have your name and the town's name. That man was simply the first.'

'Whoa, okay, let's just wait a second. Let's just take a step back.' She looked at the picture. 'This could be anyone. I'm not talking about me; I'm talking about both of us. This could be neither of us. Why...why do they think this is me or you?'

'They've been tracking me the entire trip.'

'Isn't that...? That can't be legal.'

'One would think,' he said darkly. 'Unfortunately, it is, and they've been doing it. Now, we have to act quickly and do damage control.'

It all sounded so foreign to her. Perhaps because now, she had to accept Kade was a prince. Sure, she had begun to, but it still hadn't seemed real. Not even when she was kissing him under the night sky at the beach and his bodyguard had interrupted them.

Stupidly naïve. That was what she was.

No more.

She didn't respond to him, instead taking out her phone and typing 'Prince Kade' and 'Daria'. The results came up quickly. So quickly she thought she should have done it before.

Before would have been easier. It would have prevented this from happening. She could have said no to him working for her. She could have stopped herself from becoming entangled in her attraction to him. She could have protected herself and May from whatever was about to change in her life. Because this Internet search told her things were about to change.

The picture of them kissing was one of the first to come up.

Words like 'mystery woman', 'future King', and 'hideout' popped out at her. But that didn't matter when other words were more pressing. Like her name. Her town. Her store. They mentioned May, but not by name, which was the only source of relief she had from the entire thing.

If she had done this search before all this had happened, she wouldn't be in the papers or on the Internet. May wouldn't be a daughter, four years of age, father unknown.

She regretted giving Kade privacy. She probably shouldn't have—her intentions had been noble—but what did noble matter when her daughter was in danger?

Damn it.

Her heart cracked, emotion all about spilling out of it. But she couldn't give in. She'd have to put on her rainboots, take out her umbrella, and manoeuvre through it.

'What's damage control?'

CHAPTER SEVEN

'You're not going to like it,' Kade replied.

She rolled her eyes. 'There's nothing about this situation I like. Why would damage control be any different?' She set the pictures on the counter. 'If it's going to be something I like even less than everything else, I'll need coffee.'

She moved before he could reply. She was keeping busy so she could survive the negative emotions, the reprimanding her mental voice was poised to give. It helped to shut down to the most basic of her functioning. She ignored thoughts, instincts, feelings. She only allowed logic; discussing damage control would require that.

She knew, because she had done it before.

May had been a baby then, and she hadn't known how much her mother's mistakes had affected her. That would change now—but Amari wouldn't think about it. She was May's mother. Yes, she had made another horrific mistake that affected May, but that didn't change that she had to do everything in her power to protect her daughter.

She'd leave processing her emotions about it all until after that.

'Do you want a cup?' she asked, when she felt Kade staring at her.

'No.'

'Okay.'

'Amari, I need you to listen to me.'

'I am. I will. I can listen with coffee in my hand.'

He walked into the kitchen again, and suddenly she was back on that beach, touching him. Other memories—of the awareness prickling through her the first time they were in the small kitchen together; that day on their way to Mr Kyle; countless other times when they'd come too close and were hit with that tension—walked through her mind.

No, she told them, clenching her fists, her jaw. If she shut down her mental processes, she could shut down her physical ones, too.

'I'm concerned you might drop the coffee when I tell you what you're going to have to do. Or worse—that you might throw it at me.'

'Trust me,' she said, giving him a look, 'if I was going to throw something at you, I would have done it already.' With quick movements, she poured herself a cup and took a sip. It burnt

her tongue. She didn't care. 'Okay, I'm ready.'
He shifted and she shook her head. 'No, wait,
not here.'

She pressed past him, ignoring the zing of
brushing his body, and only looked at him again
when she was safely behind the counter.

'Okay, now I'm ready. Tell me. What am I not
going to like?'

'You and May need to come with me to Daria.'

Purposefully, she didn't respond. She had
taken another sip of coffee, and she was worried
she would spit it out. That kind of thing was much
too close to the way Kade had said she was going
to react, so she would be stubborn.

She swallowed, gave herself a moment, then
said, 'We need to do *what*?'

Kade sighed. He knew this was coming. The moment Pete had woken him with the news, alerting
him to the phone call coming from the royal communication officer on how to handle the press. He
received several phone calls after that, including
from his mother, who informed him in clipped
tones that it was time he come home.

The entire time he had been thinking about
Amari. And he'd worried her reaction would affect him in the same way his mother's had.

It did.

The annoyance, the faint anger, weren't unfamiliar to him. He had encountered it many times before from his mother. But then, it was *only* his mother. She was the only person who said things to him and he knew they meant something entirely different. Now Amari seemed to share that power.

She was handling this with coolness and control, but he knew she was spitting mad inside. Because of him.

Served him right for going against his gut and kissing her.

'I know it sounds drastic—'

'It doesn't sound drastic,' she interrupted. 'It sounds insane. You want me to go to your kingdom? The one hours away from here? That's quite the commute to work every day.'

'You're not going to be able to work for a while.'

She bared her teeth at him. Bared her teeth as if she were a wild animal being cornered.

Seconds later, it eased into a thin smile.

Maybe he had imagined her snarling at him.

Maybe.

'There's no way in hell I'm not working.'

'Amari.'

He wanted to sigh her name, to convince her what he was about to outline was the best plan. He'd come up with it with Pete, with his advisors, with his mother's advisors. But he knew none of that would work, so instead he merely said her name to give himself a moment to decide how best to present the facts to her.

'What happened this morning with that reporter will be a consistent occurrence for the foreseeable future. It won't only be one. It'll be many. They will wait for you outside the store, outside your home, and once they find out where May goes to school, they'll wait there, too.'

Her face changed, but he didn't give the expression a chance to settle.

'They will go to your friends and ask them about you. It won't matter that they won't want to say anything. They will, eventually. One of them will speak out to defend you and that will become the next story. They will go through your garbage and find another story. They will dig into your history and find out everything about your family. They will…' He hesitated now, because he knew this one would be the worst. 'They will reach out to your family and ask them about you. They will offer a lot of money for those stories. And some of your family members might take it. May's father—' he cleared his throat '—May's father might take it.'

She didn't reply or interject. His gaze lowered to her hand. It was clutching her mug so tightly there was no colour in her skin. Slowly, he met her eyes.

They weren't blank, nor were they overtly emotional. They held a small amount of anger, of frustration, of fear, all coated in indignance. With a lift of her chin, stubbornness joined.

'Seems to me that'll happen whether I'm here or not.'

'Yes,' he agreed. 'But I can't protect you the way I need to here.'

'You can't protect me in the way that matters either way.'

He didn't try to argue. He understood. Her life was about to be picked apart, and she hadn't even known it would happen. There was no way to prepare her; he hadn't even considered it a possibility that he would have to prepare her.

Was it worth it? a voice whispered in his head. *Was the taste of her lips, the feel of her body, worth putting that look on her face?*

He couldn't answer.

'That might be true, Amari. It *is* true,' he corrected. 'But we have to think about it practically. And fast. Once all this happens, it'll happen fairly quickly. Your store will become invaded. You will be followed. Some of this will be reporters; others will merely be curious people. You are no longer a person to them. You're the woman a prince kissed. And they'll want to know if fairy tales are true, and, if they are, how they can make it happen for themselves.'

He wanted to move closer to offer comfort, but he didn't think she'd want that.

'I know it sounds dramatic, but it's your reality for the next few weeks at least. Until they lose interest in you, which won't happen if you're this easily accessible to them.'

'Or they'll realise, because I'm accessible to them, that I'm very boring and not someone worth reporting on or following.'

'Would you be okay to endure weeks of fear and anxiety on the *chance* that might happen?' he asked softly. When she didn't reply, he continued in the same tone. 'You have no protection in a very real sense, Amari. If you come with me to Daria, we can keep you in the palace while we figure out how to handle this.'

'Why can't you leave Pete here? Let him protect us.'

'He's not enough.'

'So send more.'

'I will,' he promised. 'Once we have better security in place here and at your home.'

'My…why?'

'Doors and alarms won't keep them away.'

'They might break into the house? The store?'

Finally he saw real fear break through. He hated it, but he needed it. Fear would keep her from doing stupid things. It would keep her safe.

'It's a possibility. We're being overly cautious.

I can send people to look after you and May, but people are fallible. Pete is the head of the royal guard and he couldn't stop people from taking pictures of us at a private beach. Guards won't be enough to keep you and May one hundred per cent safe while this blows over.'

Her tongue darted between her lips. She looked down, drew her coffee to her lips. The cup shook and, again, he wanted to comfort her. But he couldn't. Not only because she would despise him for it, but because he needed her to feel those feelings. He needed her to understand the immensity of what was about to happen.

'This is not okay, Kade,' she whispered.

'I know. I'm… I'm sorry.'

She closed her eyes. Shut them tight. Swallowed.

'I'm sorry this is your life,' she replied.

When she opened her eyes again, he saw her strength. And damn if he didn't feel his chest fill with a distinctly uncomfortable warmth.

CHAPTER EIGHT

IT ALL HAPPENED fairly quickly after that.

Amari went back to her house and packed May's clothing into a suitcase. She took May's favourite toys, the blanket she couldn't sleep without, and put that in, too. She grabbed snacks that May loved, just in case they didn't have them in Daria, and ignored the inner voice asking if she was bribing her daughter.

When she went to her own wardrobe, her productivity stalled. She stared. For a long while, she stared, because she didn't know what in her closet was appropriate to wear in a palace. After ten long minutes that didn't help her come up with an answer, she stopped thinking and threw in all her favourites. She grabbed her chargers and electronics. She put in toiletries and a towel.

Then she took a deep breath and went to fetch her kid from school.

There was a lot May had to tell her, ranging from her sleepover to the Christmas decorations she'd made that had been worth going to school on a Saturday for. Amari let her talk. It was the cowardly thing to do when she should have been explaining why they were driving to the airport. But she couldn't bear to shut down May's excitement. She was already taking May from her friends. May wouldn't see her decorations get sold at the market the following week. So she let her daughter have her excitement.

About five minutes away from the airport, May realised they weren't heading home. Amari told her what was going to happen, trying to sound reassuring. They were going to visit the Queen of a far-off land. She wanted to surprise May because Christmas in a palace was the best kind of Christmas. By the end of it, Amari had woven a tale so fantastical about royalty and Christmas that even she wanted to buy it.

But she was too old for fairy tales. The truth was that kissing Kade had been selfish and now May was paying the price for it.

You sure are making your mother proud.

Amari resisted the wince, trading it for a smile that May excitedly returned.

But the excitement quickly changed when they boarded the plane and May saw the cabin crew. She could all but see the panic of encountering strangers on May's face. Amari picked her up and held her close, but she wasn't sure if she was comforting May or herself.

'Miss Hayes, we're happy to get her settled,' a woman said, stepping forward.

'The only way that's going to happen is if she stays with me.'

Her voice was a little harder at the end, making *she stays with me* sound like a threat. Perhaps it was. She was still holding onto her control, but it was tenuous. Threats could slip through.

'That's fine,' Kade said, appearing out of nowhere.

He had the audacity to look good. He wore one of those perfectly fitted suits again, but this time it was black, his shirt white, which gave the entire look a dashing effect. She tried to keep her expression neutral, but when he smiled faintly at her, she wasn't sure she had succeeded.

'You're growling.'

No, she hadn't succeeded.

'It comes with being a parent.'

She stepped further into the plane and the crew scattered, as if Kade's presence had negated the reason for theirs. It probably had. They were likely meant to be the welcoming party. Except their guests didn't want a welcome, so why not allow the prince to take over?

The prince. It was still absolutely ludicrous.

Kade's gaze lowered to May, who had shifted her head so she could peek at him through a curtain of hair.

'Miss May,' he greeted her quietly. 'It's lovely to see you.'

May giggled, pressing her forehead back into Amari's neck.

'Remember the prince I told you about, baby?' Amari whispered into May's ear. 'That's him.'

May leaned back. 'The funny man's a prince?'

'Yes.'

May studied Kade again. 'Hello, Mr Prince.'

Kade smiled. 'Hello, Little Hayes.'

'Why you call me that?'

'Well, your mother's Big Hayes, isn't she?'

May looked at Amari. Amari shrugged. 'I am bigger than you.'

Her daughter gave it a few more seconds, then nodded. 'Okay.'

Then she put her head back into Amari's chest.

'She's not a huge fan of new things,' Amari said to Kade.

'You don't have to explain.'

'Generally, I would agree with you. But since we're imposing on your hospitality for the fore-seeable future, I think an explanation is necessary.'

Like earlier, her anger slipped through at the end. Kade's slight nod told her he had picked up on it, but he was too polite to say anything. Or perhaps he was smart enough to know he shouldn't say anything.

They got settled in the plane, which was unlike any other Amari had experienced. It was private, for one, a necessity for safety considering they were outside the kingdom and the press was determined to get to them. For another, it spoke of the kind of decadence Amari had never been comfortable with. It was partly because she'd spent her life being practical instead of decadent, and partly because she wasn't a huge fan of people who were used to decadence. They tended to see people like her as beneath them.

She knew Kade wasn't like that. But Kade had also pulled her into this world. One where all the certainty she had spent her life working for didn't matter.

Her fingers trembled as she did May's seat belt, then her own. When she looked up, Kade was watching her hands. She didn't make a fist as her gut told her to, instead letting him see what all this was doing to her. The anguish in his eyes told her she was punishing him. The satisfaction she felt told her she was trying to.

Shame immediately poured into her and she focused on May. Her daughter was having a hard time balancing her fear of the unknown and her curiosity and excitement of being on her first flight. The exhaustion of it had her asleep before dinner.

Amari ate as much of her food as she could, but that wasn't much. She wasn't hungry; she was tired. It had been a long day, and she had been keeping herself in check the entire time. She would have killed for some alone time, but that didn't happen on planes. Perhaps it didn't happen in palaces either. She sent a wish up to the heavens that that wasn't the case.

'You're not hungry?' Kade asked from his seat across the aisle.

'Not really, no.' The flight attendant took her plate away, and she offered the woman an apologetic smile. 'Please tell whoever prepared it that it isn't their fault.'

Kade waited until the woman had taken his own plate away—empty, Amari noted—before he spoke again.

'I can't imagine how difficult this must be for you.'

'I think you can,' Amari said, slumping a little. They'd put May in the bed at the back of the plane—*a bed in a plane*—so she had a little more space. 'You just don't like it.'

He made a noise of agreement.

She closed her eyes, tried to gather her thoughts. Yet somehow she was speaking before she could do it. 'Tell me what to expect.' She opened her eyes. 'Tell me what to expect when I get to your home. Will your family treat me differently because I'm a commoner who put you in this position? Will they treat me poorly?'

'They will treat you like you're my guest,' Kade said, tone hard. 'That means you'll be treated as well as any other guest.'

'You mean, I'll be treated as well as, say, the president of a country?'

Kade's expression softened. 'Better. I'll make sure of it.'

She wasn't sure why, after everything, she believed him.

'When we arrive,' Kade continued, 'you'll be taken to your room. Food can be brought up for you and May—you might be hungry then—or I can have the staff prepare something for the three of us.'

'I think eating in our room might be easier.'

He nodded. 'Tomorrow morning, you'll have breakfast with my family. We're only three—my parents and me—and they'll be perfectly polite.'

'Perfectly polite,' she repeated. 'How diplomatic of you all.'

'Well,' he said, tilting his head, 'you asked me what to expect. This is what you can expect. My family is polite and diplomatic.'

He didn't sound upset. Maybe he wasn't. Maybe she only thought he should be because she was projecting her own feelings onto the situation. She had been polite and diplomatic—for her—all day. She hadn't said what was on her mind, hadn't dealt with how she felt about any of this, and she was exhausted. She couldn't imagine what living a lifetime of it would be like.

'You're saying that when you describe your parents to people, you describe them as polite and diplomatic.'

'No,' he said with a small smile. 'But people know who my parents are. I don't have to describe them.'

'You've never spoken about your parents in casual conversation?'

'The only casual conversation I've had in the last thirty years has been with you.'

Confusion jumped from Amari's face at first. Realisation followed, and finally, sympathy.

He wasn't offended by her reaction. He knew his life was different from hers. Even if he hadn't witnessed it the past week, he would have known.

It was a good reminder. Before they reached his home. Before he got sucked into procedure and duty, and she got sucked into the same, and he saw her in the context of his life. No matter how well she did—and he had every belief that she would do well—she would be playing a part. Much as he had been playing a part in her store.

They didn't fit into one another's lives. This entire experience had illustrated that quite well.

'Okay, so you're used to having royal conversations,' Amari said. 'This isn't one of those, so you can be honest. What's your father like?'

He thought about it. 'He's...a lot like me.'

Kade smiled at that, because it was true. His father was slightly socially inept. He usually allowed his wife to take the lead, which she did flawlessly, and that had worked for them over the course of their marriage and Kade's mother's reign. When his father did solo engagements, which was rare, he wouldn't fill silences. He would wait to answer a question so he could make sure he was satisfied with his reply, even if that meant minutes. He was deliberate in a way that society wasn't used to, and he didn't have the desire to make other people feel comfortable.

He was exactly like his father in those ways, except he fought those instincts and tried to be like his mother. The result was awkward chatter, inappropriate observations.

'He's charming? Kind? Completely unable to work a coffee machine?' Amari prodded. 'There are many ways your answer could be interpreted.'

She thought him charming. It wasn't the description people used for him—the *Oops Prince* didn't exactly translate to charming—and yet here she was, using it, and not for the first time.

Perhaps she finds awkwardness charming.

Fair enough, he told that snarky inner voice.

But she had also called him kind, and, up until that point, he hadn't realised how much it meant to him that she thought him kind.

'He is kind,' Kade agreed. 'And he probably doesn't know how to work a coffee machine.'

'I understand the comparison now.'

Kade smiled. It faltered as he tried to figure out how to articulate the next part.

'My father is the youngest of five children. His mother was considered nobility in Daria, but his father was a businessman. Theirs was a chance meeting and a romantic union.'

'What did that mean for your father?'

He appreciated her ability to get to the point. 'He didn't have the "pure" nobility rearing most people marrying into the royal family had. He and my mother moved in the same circles, and she found herself drawn to him for reasons that to this day don't make sense to me. But they married.'

'Does that mean you don't have the "pureness"—' she winced as she said the word '—you're supposed to have as royalty?'

'Well.' It was all he said for a moment. 'I have a queen as a mother.'

She studied him. 'I'm struggling to follow this. It's probably because you're being diplomatic, but, unfortunately for you, I've been diplomatic all day and I can't be right now. The way you've told me all this makes you sound like you don't believe you're good enough to be royal. As if somehow being like your "regular" father means you're not like your royal mother and that means you're inadequate. Am I right?'

'I…' He trailed off, unsure how to respond. Eventually, he said, 'It does sound like that. But it's more complicated.'

'I don't think it is,' she said softly. 'You think you're faulty somehow because you're more like your father than your mother.'

He was quite speechless—and then he sighed. 'You asked me what to expect when we get to Daria? Part of it is that my father will treat you kindly. He will speak to you as he would any other, because that's his way. My mother… She will treat you politely because you are my guest. But you will get the feeling that she is not pleased with you. That's not because of you, but me. She… I suppose *she* thinks I'm faulty because I share traits with my father. He's not particularly good at social situations, which, as you might guess, is not ideal for a ruler.'

'Well,' Amari said slowly, 'she probably should have thought about that before she married him and had you. You have absolutely no control over which traits you received, Kade. But she did. It hardly seems fair that she now thinks they're faulty.'

CHAPTER NINE

HE WASN'T USED to people defending him. Certainly not against his mother. But Amari's passion on his behalf made him feel…something. It was strong and powerful and so completely foreign he knew he shouldn't engage with it. It was dangerous, getting used to having someone speak to him—about him—like that. And his mother, too.

'You probably shouldn't say that once we arrive.'

'Of course not,' she said with a roll of her eyes. 'I do have some sense of self-preservation. Even if this situation doesn't make it seem that way.'

He had no response to that. It was rather pointed, as he'd put her in the situation. It was also the truth. She should have stayed away from him; he should have stayed away from her. The fact that neither of them had made them both fools.

Except his punishment would be no different from his others. His mother's disappointment, his kingdom's disapproval. Amari's punishment was being drawn out of her life, forcing her to do the same for her daughter. It was leaving behind her home and her support system. It was leaving her job and her livelihood.

They did not compare and he deserved every pointed statement she cared to make.

They fell into silence after that. Kade imagined Amari was trying to process what had happened over the last twenty-four hours and what was to come. He was doing much the same, though he thought her process had less self-admonishment than his.

He was tired of it. Berating himself for doing the absolute worst thing in every situation. The simple solution was that he needed to stop putting himself in those situations. But that was too simple in most cases.

With Amari, he *had* put himself in the situation. But the other situations… Those were a part of his duty. He couldn't stop speaking with people or going to charity events because he wasn't good at it. He needed to become better at it.

He had been spending his life trying, to no avail.

If he was tired of it, he could only imagine his mother's frustrations. Her fears, too. She had given her entire life to Daria. She worked to establish a parliament that would keep the monarchy's power in check to appease those calling for complete liberation from the royal family. The move was widely praised, and the calls for liberation had become softer since it was clear his mother had no intention of abusing her power or disregarding parliament's decisions. She held a lot of sway in parliament, of course, and Kade had often watched her strategically guide decisions so the result would be best for the kingdom.

Daria was her life, and she must be worried Kade would destroy that.

She had never said so. She would merely chide him about his public appearances. There had been attempts to 'revitalise' his image, but he'd messed those up, too. Such as when his mother had asked him to represent her at the opening ceremony of a biennial rugby tournament. He'd gone, done his photo op, and somehow managed to mistake one of the female players as a spouse. And while he hadn't done it intentionally—she looked exactly like the spouse he had mistaken her for, down to the blue dress she wore—it had been a PR nightmare. The press had called him a misogynist, and he had spent a month wondering if it had been a mistake or if he *was* a misogynist.

His mother hadn't been impressed.

He knew she wasn't impressed with the current situation either. He had drawn attention to the fact that he wasn't in the kingdom. That wasn't entirely his fault, to be fair, but he hadn't exactly made the discovery less controversial. And because of that controversy, the news that he would be taking over from her would likely go down less smoothly in the media.

But he had a plan. The first phase had been to make sure Amari was safe. The second phase was to make things right with his mother. The third was to address the situation publicly. Phase three needed input from his secretary and the royal communications officer. Probably his mother, too.

'Hey—where's Pete?' Amari asked, looking around as if he would magically appear because she'd remembered him.

'He's still in Swell Valley.'

'Why? Shouldn't he be protecting you?'

'We've arranged for other security while he remains behind.' He hesitated, but pushed through. 'Pete is the only person who knows your business well enough to help things run while you're here.'

She gaped at him. 'You left Pete behind to look after the store?'

'He offered,' Kade replied. 'We were trying to find a solution that would be least destructive to your life. It's a good solution. He knows the basics of running the store, although I'm sure you'll hear from him quite often, and he'll get some of the other guards to help when needed. He also knows how to handle any threats should they arise, and he can oversee the security upgrades.'

'Why…why would he offer to do that?'

'He likes you.' He lifted his shoulders. 'More importantly, he respects you. Part of that respect is understanding that your business is important to you and trying to make sure it's harmed as little as possible because of this. If we're lucky, business might actually boom. I trust Pete more than anyone else to ensure that'll happen.'

She didn't speak for a while, though her lips moved, mouthing words he couldn't interpret. It fascinated him. Amari was confident and fierce, rarely stumped, but here she was. Trying to figure out what to say to him because he'd told her he'd made provisions for her business.

'If it makes you feel better, I think he also offered because he dreaded the idea of travelling in a confined space with a child.' He aimed for a light tone, hoping it would amuse her. He got a small smile.

After a moment, he said, 'I wanted to make sure this affects your life as little as possible.'

'I know,' she replied. 'I know. I just thought… I mean, my life's been pretty deeply affected.'

'I know. I'm sorry.'

'This… It doesn't make up for it, but it's pretty damn great, Kade. Thank you.'

He inclined his head in acceptance, and let the

silence slip back between them. He didn't care to fill it, knowing that they both needed time to prepare. It was funny how he knew that with her. He could sense it somehow. Yet with other people, he filled the silence with chatter. With idiocy.

It was instinctual, almost, with Amari. He could feel what she wanted and he had no idea if it was because she was special to him. He could acknowledge that without doing anything about it. But he didn't know if that was a factor, or because a week away from his mother, his responsibilities, had allowed him the space to make mistakes. He had, and the world hadn't ended.

It seemed like an important realisation to have. He should remember it.

But even as he thought it, a voice told him he wouldn't.

May was groggy when Amari woke her up once they landed. She didn't speak much, but then, May rarely did when she woke up. She had inherited her mother's unfortunate morning misery. It wasn't only confined to mornings, but after any nap. It was the one thing Amari wouldn't have minded her daughter inherit from her father.

Hank.

She shouldn't worry about him, surely. She hadn't heard from him in years. Didn't even know where he was. If reporters managed to find him, they probably deserved the story. She hadn't spoken about him to anyone in Swell Valley, and she had almost no ties in Cape Town, certainly none that would lead to him. He didn't pay child support for May, so that would lead nowhere, too. Amari hadn't had the emotional or physical capacity to go after him when he'd left. She was raising a baby alone. That was her number one priority.

Pride might have been number two.

Besides, he likely wouldn't care about what was happening with her and May anyway. But then, what did she know? Not him, that was for sure. The man *she* knew would never leave his family. So, yeah, she hadn't really known him at all.

As for her mother… Amari spoke to her more frequently. Out of that responsibility she'd honed over the years she'd looked out for herself and her mother. It was only when she got older that she realised her mother didn't need her to look out for her. She was simply not interested in living the life Amari thought she should live—she didn't care about signing parent letters or going to meetings or looking at reports. And Amari had misinterpreted that lack of interest as her mother needing help. She didn't. She did just fine without Amari. She did just fine not being a parent.

Amari didn't know if that meant she would sell

stories to reporters. She would make a call to ask her not to, but that was all she could do.

It was a relief when they drove through the thick black gates to the palace. It offered distraction. She was looking at a *real-life palace*, after all.

It surprised her. It was grand, no doubt, but it didn't look like she expected. It was more rectangular, for one. There were less pointy towers, for another. And it was old.

She had expected that, to be fair. The extent did still surprise her. It looked like history itself with the faded or stained outer walls, she couldn't tell, and the vines crawling up the sides. There were statues flanking either side of an entrance that looked like a drawbridge, though there was no water underneath. Instead, there were flowers. Beds of red and white and blue.

The minute she stepped inside the palace, her hold on May tightened. The floor was an old, gorgeous wood that fitted perfectly with the pale gold walls. A carpet of the same gold formed a path to a door to their right, and Amari realised they were merely in a reception hall of some kind. She already felt deeply out of place in the reception hall with its ridiculously large paintings of what she assumed were the kingdom and previous sovereigns.

She didn't get a chance to examine any of the

pictures—or anything about the hall beyond her initial observations, really—when Kade strode ahead of her through the doors to their right. She followed, not because she thought she should, but because she didn't know what else to do. No one beyond a tall woman who looked to be a decade or so older than her was there. Kade introduced the woman as his secretary, Matilda, but the older woman didn't say one word to Amari. Amari didn't know if it was a slight or protocol, but she thought it best to stick to the one person who treated her as if she was a person.

For now.

Well, yes, thank you, she told that helpful inner voice.

Because she definitely wanted to think about the fact that she was stepping into an entirely different world with only one ally. And she had to protect May, too. She could have done without her inner voice trying to sabotage her.

The room Kade had entered proved to be even more splendid than the reception hall. This one had actual gold on the walls. It formed frames of two large pictures, both in the same position on either wall. One was of a beautiful woman whose features reminded her of Kade, though there was no one thing Amari could point out that they shared. On the other wall was a picture of a gorgeous man. In him, she could clearly see Kade's lips and eyes.

Glass stretched between the two walls, covered in a gauzy material, though thick blue curtains hung on either side. In the room itself was the most expensive-looking furniture she had ever seen. Not in the middle of the room, but on the sides of a large blue carpet. As if they wanted to highlight the carpet. While she knew the value of a good carpet, and this one looked pretty great, she didn't know if it warranted centrepiece status.

She didn't understand any of it, but as she watched Kade turn to her in the middle of the room, she understood that he fitted here. It suited him as well as the suits tailored for him did.

For the first time, she thought maybe she *didn't* really understand him. Not if he fitted so perfectly in a place she could barely make sense of.

'It's a lot, I know.'

He grimaced as he said it, and she shook her head.

'It's beautiful.'

'Grand.'

'They're not mutually exclusive.'

He smiled, as if saying anything more would be admitting to something he didn't think he should. 'I'll show you to your rooms, and then we'll call down to the kitchen and get food sent up for you.'

'Oh—you don't have to show us to our rooms,' she said. 'I'm sure you have more important things to do. Someone else can do it.'

'I'd like to do it,' he said gently, firmly. Those same things—gentleness, firmness—fluttered in his eyes. He needed this. He needed to do this for them, and, though she shouldn't be trying to make him feel better when her entire life was out of place because of him, she nodded.

'Thank you.'

She followed him, her arms growing weary after carrying May for so long. May let out a little cry every time Amari tried to put her down. She didn't blame her daughter. If someone could carry her around, protect her, comfort her right in this moment, she wouldn't say no.

Eventually, Kade stopped in front of a large door. He pushed it open and gestured for her to go inside. Her feet sank into the carpet when she did, and she barely stopped herself from gasping. The room was gigantic, probably the size of the entire flat she still spent most of her income paying for back home. There was a four-poster bed in the middle of the room, a dresser opposite it, a cupboard along another wall, and a large window opposite that. A window seat had been built below the glass, and it looked as comfortable as the bed did. It also had a much better view—the ocean.

'Wow,' she breathed. She walked to the window, nudged May. 'Look over there, baby.'

May just clung tighter. Amari sighed and turned to Kade.

'It's lovely. Thank you.'

'We thought you might want to sleep with May, but, if that situation changes, we've prepared the adjoining room for her.'

'She'll stay here with me.'

He nodded. 'The bathroom's through there, and you can call down—' he walked to the phone next to the dresser '—whenever you need to and someone will respond. The list of numbers is here.' He tapped a panel next to the phone. 'I've had my number added to the list as well. Any time you need me, night or day, please call.'

'Thank you.'

'I know it's a lot,' he said, stepping forward. 'I… I'm sorry.'

'We're in it now, Kade,' she replied, though her heart was beating fast and she felt as if she needed the apology. As if she deserved it. 'There's no point in doing anything but make the best out of it.'

He studied her, but nodded. 'Would you like me to call down for anything?'

'I know it's not fancy or anything, but we could do with some burgers and fries.' She dipped her head to gesture to May. 'It's her favourite. I think she could do with some comfort.'

'Of course. I'll make sure you get it in the next thirty minutes. It should give you enough time to freshen up.' His brow knitted as he looked at May. 'Is she okay?'

Amari rubbed May's back. 'Like you said, it's a lot. But she'll be fine. We'll both be fine,' she added.

She wasn't sure if she was reassuring Kade or herself.

'Darling,' Queen Winifred said when he eventually joined his parents for a meal.

He wasn't ashamed to admit he'd stalled. He'd arranged for Amari and May's dinner, been to his own rooms to freshen up and had taken his sweet time doing so. But he had needed the space. He wanted to erase the memory of Amari's tight expression as she told him she and May would be fine. He wanted a moment to breathe before he found his mother and that emotion he felt with Amari started to weigh even more.

'Mother,' he said. 'You look lovely.' He brushed a kiss on his mother's cheek, before moving to his father and shaking his hand. 'Father.'

'Son.'

Without saying anything else, he took his seat opposite his mother. It wasn't strange any more that they sat at a small table. A six-seater liberally set to accommodate the three of them. His father sat at the head of the table, his mother at the side, and Kade opposite his mother.

It was late for them to be eating, but Kade knew they'd arranged it this way to talk. He didn't say anything as the waitstaff set his meal in front of him. He waited.

He didn't have to wait for long.

'Quite the mess you've found yourself in, isn't it?' his mother said, swirling around her wine in a glass.

'It isn't the first time,' he answered, since that was what she was implying.

Winifred gave an impatient sigh. 'I wanted you to have the time you asked for to recuperate, Kade. To prepare. I wanted you to have your freedom. But this—'

'Is hardly something we could have anticipated.'

'Are you in love with her?'

Good thing he hadn't started eating. He would have choked, and that would have displeased his mother even more. '*No*, Mother. It was a kiss.'

'It looked to be a little more than a kiss.'

He made a disgusted noise. 'Please, don't.'

'If you can't keep your hands to yourself on a public beach, then you can hardly be upset with me—and the world, for that matter—for react-ing to it.'

'I didn't—' He broke off. 'It was a private beach. We're looking into suing the reporter for trespassing.'

His mother snorted. It wasn't something she would have ever done in public. She rarely did it in front of them. But apparently this situation warranted a snort.

'It won't make a difference.'

'It will to me.' It would give him back some measure of control, even if it was merely the illu-sion of it. 'Regardless, I couldn't anticipate that a kiss I shared with a woman I respect would make it onto every newspaper in Daria.'

'A woman you respect?' Winifred repeated. 'You're not in love, but you respect her.' He didn't answer. 'That's worse, possibly.'

He didn't speak for a moment. Even after tak-ing a beat, he said, 'I don't think I want to know how you've come to that conclusion.'

'Love is passion,' his mother said, as if he had, indeed, asked. 'It burns hot, but it burns fast. Usually, it fizzles out. Oh, I didn't mean you, dear,' she told her husband, Deacon, when he looked up. 'Sometimes, if you're lucky, it lasts.'

'But if I had been in love with Amari, it wouldn't have been the kind that lasts.'

'Respect,' Winifred continued, and he didn't

know if she was ignoring him or agreeing with him, 'is built on a much sturdier foundation. You feel responsible for this woman now, which I already assumed considering she's here in your kingdom, distracting you from the fact that you're about to become King.'

'Nothing could distract me from the fact that I'm about to become King.'

'And that's where you underestimate having this woman here.'

He exhaled. 'Mother, I put her in this situation. She isn't safe in her home because of me. I can hardly have her and her daughter in danger because of something I did.'

'Did you coerce her into kissing you?'

'Of course not.'

'And you were honest about who you are?'

'Yes.'

'Then she's put herself into this situation just as much as you have.'

'You and I both know it isn't as simple as that.'

Winifred sighed, and suddenly looked every inch of her seventy years. It was plausibly because of her illness, but Kade couldn't help but wonder if it was him. Was he making his mother age? Was her concern about him making her feel worse?

It was self-indulgent, and a part of him knew that. But he wished he knew for sure. He wished he knew what it would be like to make his mother proud, and not feel as though she had to coach him through every decision he made.

'I'm not going to claim that this isn't a bad situation,' he said. The least he could do was be honest. 'I know bringing Amari and May here complicates things. But being responsible is part of being King. Making sure people are safe is part of being King.' He paused. 'She might not be a part of this kingdom, but I've inadvertently drawn her into this. She has a right to be offered those things just as much as anyone else in this kingdom.'

His mother opened her mouth to reply, but his father laid a hand over hers. They exchanged a look, before Deacon looked at him. 'You're right. And we're proud of you for it.'

The words would have meant more if they'd come from his mother, but he told himself to take the win. He might not have acted like an adult before, getting himself into this mess, but he was now. And it meant something to him that his father saw it. His mother would get on board or she wouldn't, but there was nothing he could do about that.

That didn't mean he wouldn't try.

Picking up his utensils, he told his parents his plan.

CHAPTER TEN

AMARI DIDN'T DARE slip out of her room as she wanted to that night. She was afraid she would get lost. She was afraid May would wake up, see that she wasn't there, and panic.

But she couldn't sleep, so she spent the night on that wonderful window seat, looking out at the magnificent garden, at the ocean in the distance.

It helped clarify some things. Like the fact that she had been blaming Kade when she, too, had a part in what had happened between them. It was the easier option, blaming him. She didn't have to think too deeply about how she had made the same mistakes he had. They'd kissed and they both knew they shouldn't have. For their own reasons. But they had. Because... Well, for a number of reasons. Including that the moment on the beach had been *magical.*

The sky had slowly been turning to night; stars had begun flickering down on them; waves had crashed at their feet; and Kade had looked every inch the prince he was. Tall and stately, that intensity shining through his eyes, aimed at her, as if she were the only thing he wanted to look at, to see. Anyone could have fallen for that.

Except it hadn't been anyone. It had been her. She was the reason she and May had to move away from the community who had welcomed them with open arms. She was the reason she no longer trusted that community to keep them safe. Someone had told that reporter where to find her. And though she didn't blame whoever it was, she simply couldn't believe that if she'd stayed, people would have protected her. That was on her more than it was them. And she felt as if she had lost something pivotal, something precious, because of it.

She had projected her frustration about it onto Kade, too. She had even used him as the reason May was so quiet. He'd forced them to come to the palace. But Amari had agreed to it. Amari was the reason May's life had been upended, and that was the real reason May was acting like this. She didn't do well with new things. It was something they were working on, as much as one could work on something like that with a four-year-old, but this was…this was too fast. It was throwing her into the deep end of a pool and expecting her to swim.

They had no choice though. Not any more. So

Amari would jump in with May and hold her up until she learnt how to swim.

There was a knock on the door.

Amari glanced at May, who was clutching her favourite teddy and looking out of the window. Amari had succeeded in directing her interest to the boats they could see in the distance. May was currently trying to figure out what the boats were doing.

'Hi,' she said when she opened the door to Kade.

'Good morning.'

His voice was smooth and deep and she hated that it soothed something inside her. She hated that he looked as he had that night on the beach; princely and handsome and downright irresistible. She hated that, looking like that, he reminded her that kissing him wasn't as simple as saying she had been irresponsible. There had been more to it. Attraction and a pull she couldn't explain. She hadn't felt anything that strong before. Not even with Hank.

She hated it.

No, you don't.

And that was part of the problem.

'How did you sleep?' he asked, all concern. Really, it made her want to hit him.

Or kiss him.

'As well as expected,' she answered vaguely.

He narrowed his eyes. 'Why do I feel like that means not well at all?'

'Does it matter?'

'To me, very much so.'

She took a shaky breath. *You hate this, remember?* she told herself. She lied to herself.

'I didn't sleep.'

He stepped forward. 'Is there anything I can do?'

'No.' He was in her space, messing with her head with that scent of his. 'There's something I should do though.' She took a deliberate step back. 'Apologise. This situation isn't your fault. Well, not only.'

She gave him a small smile. A controlled smile. It would give her some power back. She would be able to pretend her emotions weren't shifting inside her, trying to get to him.

'I... I appreciate that.'

'You seem surprised.'

'No, no. It's not that. I just... Well, my mother said the same thing last night.'

Amari stared. 'I'm glad she and I will be starting off on the right foot, then.'

He smiled. 'I know you're being sarcastic, but the fact that you agree with her and said so without her prodding bodes well for your relationship.'

She snorted. 'I doubt you can call whatever

will happen between your mother and me a relationship.'

He angled his head. 'Don't sound so sure.' Without pausing, he nodded towards May. 'How is she doing?'

Amari sighed. 'She's scared. It's a lot of new, and I…' She trailed off. She was about to say something corny, like she wished she hadn't put May in this situation. Like she should have been a better mother, and that was why she was taking responsibility for this situation. It had nothing to do with him. She settled for, 'I wish I had something to distract her with.'

'I might be able to help with that,' he said mischievously. 'May I?'

'She might not respond, but you're more than welcome to try.'

He walked into the room and sat down on the bed opposite the window seat. Amari thanked the heavens she'd been trained into making up a bed in the mornings. Something about him sitting there already felt intimate. She could only imagine what it would be like if he were sitting on an unmade bed, as if he'd spent the night there.

You need to stop this, she told herself, and tried to listen.

'May, do you remember…?' Amari hesitated. She was about to say Kade, but that felt wrong.

Prince Kade sounded too formal, too. 'Do you remember Uncle Kade?' she asked with a grimace.

Kade glanced at her in confusion. She wrinkled her nose. Gave him a shrug. May turned towards them and prevented any further communication.

'The funny man,' May said without any preamble.

Amari walked closer with a smile. 'Yes.'

May nodded.

Kade took over. 'Remember how you gave us letters to send to Father Christmas last week?'

May eyed him suspiciously, but nodded.

'I think if you wrote another one, we could get it to him quicker from here.'

May frowned.

'You should come with me. You and your mom,' Kade added quickly, with a furtive glance her way, 'and see what I mean.'

May looked at Amari. Amari nodded and held out her hand, and after a long pause—during which May studied Kade suspiciously a while longer—she shimmied off the couch and went to Amari, taking her hand.

'Lead the way, Uncle Kade,' Amari said, a lightness she hadn't felt since they'd left Swell Valley dancing inside her chest at the look he gave her.

But he didn't protest, merely leading the way

through the door into the gigantic hall. Amari picked up more of it now that she was less afraid, and perhaps because it was daylight, too. It looked a lot like a hotel with the pictures up in frames on the walls and small tables with fresh flowers at different intervals. There were more expensive things on the walls the deeper they got into the palace. Gold accents, expensive artworks, things Amari couldn't entirely wrap her brain around.

It was a bit of a relief when Kade stopped in front of a door. It was larger, stretching over her head. The wood looked ancient.

She lifted her brows. 'Are you taking us to a dungeon?'

He widened his eyes down at May, who looked up at him expectantly. 'No, of course not. Why would you say that?'

She laughed at the nerves. Kade's and her own. She was pretty sure he had taken them to a dungeon. 'It was an innocent question. May's read about dungeons in her fairy-tale books. She knows it's where they keep the princesses.'

She winked. Kade visibly relaxed, then lowered to his haunches. 'There aren't any princesses here,' he said seriously. 'But there is… well…would you like to see?'

May's grip on Amari's hand tightened, but she nodded. Amari tried not to let the little exchange do anything to her heart, and watched as Kade knocked on the door. Seconds later, it opened.

She wasn't sure who gasped louder: she or May.

The room was massive. There was the tallest Christmas tree she had ever seen in one corner. It went up to the roof, which had been covered in snowflakes. They were decorations, but she half expected to feel the ice prickle her skin. An ice slide took up most of the room, and since almost everything leading to the slide, as well as everything around it, was padded, she assumed it had been created with the safety of kids in mind. Near the tree was a table with blank paper and crayons. A man in an elf uniform stood just beyond it with a patient expression, as if his entire purpose in life were to play an elf. There was also an elf on the other side of the tree, which she now noticed had a great number of Christmas presents beneath it, and a few more elves near the start of the slide. Opposite the table was a fairly simple jungle gym, not at all Christmas decorated, though, by being in this Christmas-themed place, it seemed like a Christmas jungle gym.

Amari looked down at May and smiled at the look of awe.

Kade lowered to his haunches again. 'This is where we send our letters to Father Christmas.

We write them over there—' he pointed at the table '—before giving them to that elf, who will help us with the address and make sure it's in an envelope. Then, we go over there—' he pointed to the slide '—with them, tuck them into our pockets, and slide down until we get there.' He pointed to the end of the slide.

She hadn't noticed before, but the end of the slide led to a small door with a slot in it.

'We pop the letters in there and trust that the elves on the other side send them to Father Christmas.'

As he said it, fingers in white gloves popped through the slot, wiggling, as if they were looking for something. May gasped and Amari bit down so she didn't laugh. It was simply joyful. It was *wonderful*.

'We write as many letters as we want, but we also use the slide even if we don't have letters.' He dropped his voice. 'We had to get special permission for that, but it was worth it. But don't tell the other Christmas postal stations.'

Christmas postal stations.

Whoever came up with it was brilliant.

'We had a jungle gym set up here in case any of the children didn't feel like using the slide. We don't force anyone to do something they don't want to in Daria,' he continued matter-of-factly. 'And we also have some hot-chocolate stations over there, marshmallows over there, and some Christmas biscuits over there. But first we have breakfast, of course.'

He straightened then, throwing Amari an apologetic look. 'I probably shouldn't have mentioned the hot chocolate before the breakfast part,' he said under his breath.

'Is it possible for that hot chocolate to be served with pancakes?' Amari asked.

'Yes.'

'How about some fruit with those pancakes?'

'That's exactly how the…um…the elves do it here.'

Amari's lips curved, but she kept the smile in. 'Well, then, it sounds like breakfast is all sorted here at the Christmas postal station. What do you say, May?'

May stayed silent for a while, then she looked at them both and gave them the biggest smile Amari had seen.

'Can we write a letter, Mama?' she asked.

Amari laughed. 'After breakfast, honey.'

With a disappointed sigh, May took Amari's hand and led her to the hot-chocolate station. They'd taken a few steps towards it when May turned around and asked Kade, 'Are you coming?'

After several blinks, Kade nodded. 'I would love to.'

* * *

'I'm sorry we didn't get to eat with your parents,' Amari said.

It was a while after breakfast, and the two of them had settled in to watch May take her second slide down. The child was having the time of her life. It was such a leap from how she had looked when they'd arrived or when Kade had seen her this morning. He felt no insignificant amount of pride that he'd helped put that smile on her face.

'We should make it in time for tea,' Kade replied.

'Oh?' Amari straightened in her seat. He'd had the adult-sized comfortable chairs brought in for them. Even he was feeling relaxed. 'I can't imagine they're thrilled I didn't make breakfast. Or that I pulled you away from it.'

'You didn't pull me away from anything,' he said. 'I chose to be here.'

Though in some ways, she was right. He was choosing her company rather than that of his parents, or his responsibilities. In the grand scheme of things, carving out a few hours in the morning for himself wouldn't hurt anyone. But he was already on thin ice. He should be out there doing damage control, or strategising, or preparing the press release he'd scheduled for later that day.

Instead, he was sitting in a comfortable chair

next to Amari, enjoying the sound of her child's laughter.

'That's probably the truth,' she said quietly, 'but I think you might be choosing me as an excuse.'

He laughed lightly. 'You weren't going to be polite enough to not call me out on it, were you?'

She clucked her tongue. 'When have you ever known me to be polite, Kade?'

'It should be annoying.'

'But it's not.'

'No.'

They smiled at one another. It was a simple smile—until it wasn't. Until it became more. Until it became a bond, a symbol of that pull between them. It flared with attraction, spun with heat, and soon they weren't smiling any more, just staring at one another.

Kade didn't know what was happening in Amari's head, but he was thinking about their kiss. The sweet taste of her lips, the slick heat of her tongue, the gentle curve of her waist. It had tortured him that night, the memory of their kiss. Not because he was thinking about how he shouldn't have done it, but because he was thinking about how much he wanted to do it again. This time, he didn't want to be stopped. He didn't want to stop at all. He wanted to feel the curve of her breasts, her thighs. He wanted her heat, her sighs, her moans until neither of them could breathe.

Amari looked away first, cursing as she did.

'You can't do that,' she said, her voice barely above a whisper.

'What?' His voice was no better.

'You know what I'm talking about.' The words were harsh. 'You can't look at me like you want me in your bed. That's what got us in this situation in the first place.'

'I thought you were taking responsibility for this situation.'

'I am.' She gave him a look. 'I didn't say I don't want to be in that bed. I do. And that's the problem.'

Kade opened his mouth, but found that he didn't have anything to say to that. Largely because she had caused a meltdown in his brain with the image of her in his bed. He hadn't allowed himself to indulge in that fantasy, and knowing she wanted to be there was…a lot to process.

She shook her head. 'There's no future for this. It's best I don't end up there.'

'Why?' he asked.

It was a stupid question. He knew why there was no future. He was about to be King. He had enough on his plate with that, and he wasn't even factoring his mother into the equation. He wanted to make her proud. He wanted her to feel at peace with him being King. He had a plan to get her there, but that plan would mean nothing if he was distracted by a woman.

Yet here he was, distracted by a woman.

'You don't need an answer to that,' Amari said, infinitely wiser than he was. 'But I'm going to answer you anyway. Beyond the fact that you're about to be King, your mother is ill. You probably want to be there for her as much as you can. How will that be possible with me in the mix?'

'My mother has the best healthcare in the world,' he surprised himself by answering. 'I can't do much for her beyond support her and try to make her proud. The former she knows she has. Unwaveringly.'

When he didn't continue, she said, 'And the latter?'

'I've told you my struggles, Amari,' he replied after a moment. 'Our situation hasn't done anything to soothe her fears when it comes to me and ruling this kingdom. I can't imagine the abdication will be easy on her in general, but with this, with me, it must be particularly hard.'

She stayed silent for a while. 'You told me she hasn't said anything about it. About your struggles, I mean. Is that true?'

'She's mentioned it.'

'That she's disappointed in you?'

'That she would like me to try harder.'

'And you've been interpreting that as her disappointment?'

'How else would you interpret it?'

'Well, if I was telling May that, it would probably be because I see her potential, and I think she's not living up to it.'

'How is that different from disappointment?'

'It's called raising a child, Kade. It's called support. It's knowing that, perhaps, they're not doing what you know they can do and trying to guide them into doing what you know they can do.'

'I…she's… She's not…'

'But how do you know that?' she pressed. 'You've never asked her. You've assumed.'

'I know what I'm—'

'You never truly know what the other person is thinking unless you talk to them,' she interrupted, and something about how she said it made him think she wasn't only talking about him.

It was fair. He could hardly argue with that. It was completely reasonable for him to ask his mother about what she thought about him and his abilities. He had never thought about it before. Now that he did… Well, he wasn't sure he wanted to know the answer.

Would it be easier if she told him she was disappointed in him rather than him assuming it? And what if she didn't say she was disappointed in him? What if…what if she thought he wasn't living up to his potential, as Amari said? Maybe part of living up to that potential meant asking his mother for guidance. Maybe she was waiting for him to acknowledge that he couldn't rule alone. That he needed help.

'I can't believe the children of the palace get to come here every Christmas,' Amari mused out loud.

'They don't,' he replied distractedly, still thinking about whether she was right.

'What do you mean?'

'I had this done when I knew you were coming. It's not a standard thing.'

'You mean…you mean you did this for May?'

Something in her voice had him focusing on her again. 'Yes.'

'All this…for her?'

He was more hesitant this time. 'Yes.'

'Kade…it's…this is…wow.'

'That doesn't sound like a good wow.'

'I'm still trying to figure out whether it is a good wow.' She exhaled shakily.

'Should I apologise?'

'I… I don't know.'

He waited for more.

'I feel like I should be upset with you for this, but I can hardly blame you for this extravagance. I mean, look at your home. It's beautiful and expensive and grand. Of course you're going to make this Christmas postal station as beautiful and expensive and grand as the rest of your home.'

He still didn't say anything.

'But…this is a lot. I'm not saying it's bad. Clearly not.' She gestured to May, laughing as they pushed her down the slide once more. 'But maybe…maybe May shouldn't be the only one enjoying this. Maybe you should let your staff bring their children here, too. Maybe it wouldn't seem so extravagant if it wasn't only for May.'

He almost spoke then, to say that it *was* only for May. He had only been thinking of May's smile, which he had really only seen twice in his life, and yet it seemed quite important to him. Well—fine, he hadn't only been thinking of May. He had been thinking of Amari, too. He had been thinking about seeing her smile. About making her daughter happy so she could be happy, too.

But this was the kind of person she was. She had done the same thing when she'd suggested the royal family offer gifts to their people instead of the people offering them gifts. She thought about how others could benefit. Especially those who weren't in positions of power.

He took a steadying breath. 'You're right. I'll have Matilda inform the staff.'

She sat back with a nod of approval. Then she sighed.

'This life is very different from mine, isn't it?'

He looked up and saw Matilda gesture to him from the door.

'I suspect it is.' He paused. 'And we'll have confirmation of it soon. It's time for tea with my parents.'

CHAPTER ELEVEN

AMARI HAD NEVER met a queen before. She had never thought it an experience she'd want until now, when she was actually meeting a queen and she had no idea what she was doing.

Matilda had told her to curtsy, had shown her how, but Amari still felt as if she'd messed up. Although based on what Kade told her, it was highly possible that Queen Winifred's expression of faint disapproval was one she carried with her wherever she went.

If Amari *had* met a queen before, maybe she would have known that with more certainty. Then again, she had no desire to feel inept twice. So perhaps meeting one, if slightly disapproving, queen was enough.

Kade's father was much more relaxed. Or perhaps she merely felt relaxed with him because Deacon was so much like Kade. That wasn't a good admission, since she shouldn't have felt relaxed with Kade either. He was a prince. He built Christmas stations for her kid. He made sure her store was taken care of and they were safe even though he didn't have to.

He was kind and attractive and insecure mixed with the deepest sincerity and she should not have felt relaxed with him.

Still, she sought his eyes when she sat down. Looked for his reassurance. When she got it, her heart stopped beating so erratically.

This is not good, a voice in her head whispered.

No, duh, she whispered back, and tried to focus.

'Amari, Kade tells me you have a daughter.'

'Yes, Your Majesty.'

'Oh, please.' Winifred waved her hand. 'Call me ma'am.'

'Mother,' Kade chided, but Amari laughed.

'Ma'am it is.' They shared a smile. Amari had not expected that. She cleared her throat. 'I do have a daughter. She's four years old and the love of my life.'

'Kade seems quite fond of her, too.'

'Mother.'

This time it was a warning. Winifred merely lifted an eyebrow, but she didn't say any more.

'I'd be happy for you to meet her,' Amari said. 'She's at the Christmas station. Kade assures me she's safe, though I am currently resisting the urge to check on her.'

'You can check on her,' Kade said gently.

She offered him a smile. 'She'll be okay. I know she'll be okay. It's just… It's part of being a parent.'

Amari didn't miss the look Winfred and Deacon exchanged. She didn't know what it meant. Or maybe she did, but she didn't want to think about it.

'Tell me about your life in Swell Valley.'

This from Deacon. He looked sincere, and she told him, but she felt uncertain the entire time. It was like meeting the parents of a boyfriend. The parents who apparently didn't like her. Or tolerated her, because she was dating their only son and they had no choice but to support his decision even though they didn't particularly like her. The worst part about it was that she wasn't dating their son. He wasn't her boyfriend, except how were they to know that? The only thing they knew about her for sure was that she'd kissed their son and turned the news of his impending rule into a dating show.

Oh. Yeah. She wouldn't like her either.

'My store is essentially a trinket store,' she continued nervously. 'I source my inventory locally, which involves the community and really garners support from them. It's…um…it's great.'

Yeah, it sounds great.

'It's really quite magnificent,' Kade said. 'The community love her because she supports them. She gets quite a lot of traffic from out-of-town visitors since she's on the edge of town, so both locals and foreigners support her.'

'Oh, I—'

'You're being modest,' he interrupted. 'And while that's a fine quality, you should brag here.'

'Kade,' she said, shifting a little. 'Thank you, but you're making it sound more important than it is.'

'I am not,' he said, rearing back as if she insulted him. 'My parents, out of everyone, understand the value of making the community feel as though they're a part of something.'

There was a beat where no one spoke. It was fine that Amari didn't, but she suspected Kade wanted his parents to jump in and agree with him. Their silence didn't seem like a slight to her, though she was sure it probably was. It felt like a slight to Kade, who was doing his best to make her comfortable and his parents weren't exactly playing along.

'Thank you.' She spoke directly to Kade. 'I believe you, and I'm saying thank you.'

His eyes twinkled back at her. He was saying *thank you*, too, because she was seeing him in a way his parents didn't. Or she was validating him in a way his parents didn't.

Well, he had done the same for her. She had never looked at her store in the way he'd described. Sure, on some level she knew that including local products was something special. But it had made her a part of the community in a way she hadn't expected. She was quite proud of that, even if she hadn't acknowledged it before. Hearing him say it allowed her to say that it was…significant.

'Well, it sounds like you're doing quite well, Amari,' Winifred said, her tone no less cool and distant. But there was something more there. She couldn't put her finger on it, but it was there. 'Which really begs the question as to why you would risk it all by kissing my son.'

Amari sucked in her breath even as Kade snapped a reproach at his mother. But Winifred paid him no mind. Her sharp eyes were on Amari.

She remembered that Kade had said his mother had told him Amari played a part in this, too. It seemed like a strange time to remember it until she realised her brain was trying to tell her something. Seconds later, it clicked.

'You're wondering if I kissed him because he's a prince.'

'Yes.'

'Amari, you don't have to do this.'

'I know,' she told Kade, but she didn't look

away from Winifred. 'I didn't believe he was a prince, ma'am. I thought he was in trouble and telling me a story about being a prince so I wouldn't ask questions.'

She debated how honest she wanted to be. Thought about how worried she was about May all the time. If Kade were her son, she'd be worried about her intentions, too. So she went with the entire truth.

'There was a time I was in trouble, too. I was a young mother, abandoned by her husband, with no support system, and I despised the idea of anyone asking me questions. So I didn't ask Kade questions, though he was perfectly upfront about who he really was.'

'You didn't do an Internet search?'

'It felt like a violation,' she replied. 'He told me to, and yet it still felt like a violation. Again, this is likely because of my own experiences.'

The next part would be harder. She took a breath.

'If someone had looked into me in that way, I'm not sure what they would have found. But even the idea of it terrified me. I had irrational fears that it would somehow lead my husband, who'd left May and me, to us. I was afraid he would want us back or that he'd try to take May away.' She avoided Kade's eyes. 'I thought I was affording Kade a privacy and freedom from those

But this was easier. And less weird, he supposed.

'Why…um…why did you knock?'

'I was wondering if you'd like to take a walk in the garden.'

'Oh.' Genuine surprise. 'Oh. Um… I shouldn't leave May alone.'

'I can have someone come up and stand outside the door. If she wakes up, they'll call me and we'll have you back in a matter of minutes.'

'That's ridiculous. I can't have someone guard the door as if…' She trailed off.

'As if you're in a palace? As if you're royalty? As if we have countless people whose job it is to guard something precious?'

She narrowed her eyes. 'Your snarkiness doesn't mean I'm going to say yes.'

'Maybe not. But it should.'

He grinned. She bit her lower lip, rolled her eyes and said, 'Fine. Do I look okay to go out like this? I feel like I need to watch everything I wear. What if someone sees us and thinks you're hanging out with the help? There's nothing wrong with that, of course,' she added hastily, 'but I can't imagine it'll make things easier for you. First you kiss a shopkeeper who happens to be a divorced single mother, then you stroll in the garden with the help.'

Divorced.

He set the information aside, just as he had

fears I would have loved when I was that terrified.' She paused. 'And on top of all this, doing an Internet search felt like an admission that I believed him. It was too ridiculous to even consider.'

She tried to end it on a lighter note, but she didn't think she achieved it.

No one interrupted her, not even to ask a question. She had a rapt audience; she had to continue whether she wanted to or not. But she could make it concise, so she jumped right to the point.

'I wasn't thinking about Kade as a prince when I kissed him, ma'am. I was thinking about him as a man. He's…um… Well, he's an impressive man.' Her face heated, but she continued. 'I was attracted to him, and after a glass of wine there seemed to be fewer reasons to resist that attraction.' She met Kade's eyes. 'He and I both know it was a mistake.' When something flickered in his eyes, she looked back to his mother. 'But making mistakes is human. We handle them. Learn from them. Try to do better.' She exhaled.

The silence this time didn't seem as intimidating as before. Still, it didn't make her feel comfortable. She took her tea, cool now, and drank as much of it as she could. It wasn't polite, she didn't think. She might have even broken a few royal protocols. But she had exposed her soul to royalty and it made her thirsty.

'Seems you have your answer, Mother,' Kade said eventually. 'Any other questions you'd like to ask Amari that you could easily get answers from me for?'

Winifred's expression went from pensive to sharp. 'Don't sass me, son.'

Kade narrowed his eyes. 'I would respectfully request you offer me and Amari the same courtesy.'

She shouldn't have been amused, but she was. Royals even *argued* politely. When things had eventually got bad enough between her and her mother—and her and Hank, for that matter—there wasn't much politeness.

It was new, sitting there, watching them be formal, but something about what she had said, and the fact that she had said it, made her less uncomfortable. When Winifred sat back and asked her about her bestselling product, she answered as she would have with anyone else.

It wasn't right that he found Amari more attractive because of how expertly she handled his mother during tea. The best part was that she wasn't handling his mother at all. She was being honest, treating his mother as she would any other person, and something about it had earned his mother's respect. He saw it the moment his mother looked at him after Amari spoke.

It made him want to kiss Amari until neither of them could speak. Which was a foolish wish, yet he was still devising a plan to make it happen.

He didn't stop to think about the ethics of it. Or he did, but he told himself it would be fine. They were both adults, and it would only be a kiss. And nothing would happen if Amari didn't want it to.

He hoped it wouldn't come to that.

'Aren't there other things for you to do with your time than escort me back and forth?' she asked when she opened her door.

'Yes,' he agreed. 'And I've done them. I have this afternoon to myself.'

She looked over her shoulder, then slipped through the door, closing it behind her. 'We do, too. It was an exhausting day of sliding for May, and she was so testy at my suggestion for a nap. And now she's out like a light.'

'Did I wake her with my knock?'

'What do you think out like a light means?'

He smiled. He hadn't planned this. In fact, he intended on taking May with them. He wasn't proud of it, but he was going to distract her by showing her the swing his parents had put in for him when he was a child. It was magnificent, and had kept him busy for hours. He had already put one of the elves on standby to supervise. And he only needed minutes to steal a kiss.

when she'd mentioned during tea with his parents that her husband had left her. There was a stack of information about her and her past on the desk in his office, but somehow it felt like a betrayal to look at it. He wanted to know about her past, about her, from *her*. He wanted to get to know her as anyone else would.

'For one, no one will see us. The garden is entirely secure. And second...'

He let his eyes lower, taking her in. It wasn't what she meant when she asked if she looked okay, but he couldn't resist the opportunity. She wore a plain white cotton dress with big brown buttons down the middle. It had capped shoulders, lowering into a respectable V at her chest. The brown of her skin was complemented by the gold necklaces she wore. Three layers: one that hugged her neck, the second lying slightly lower, with the third scooping until the edge of the material of her dress. Her shoes were gold, too, matching the necklace, and her earrings were bright orange mixed with gold, dangling midway down her neck.

It was all very simple, including the curls she had tied up to the top of her head. It created the most alluring picture. Simple and alluring were excellent descriptions of her.

When he met her eyes again, saw the blush at her cheeks, he smiled. 'You look beautiful.'

'You took so long to come up with "beautiful"?' she grumbled, but she pushed a curl behind her ear.

'I have other words, but I'm almost certain you wouldn't want to hear them.'

She muttered something that sounded suspiciously like 'too late', but she was talking after that and he didn't get the chance to ask.

'If you wouldn't mind calling someone you trust to guard the door, I'd appreciate that.'

He did so immediately, and they waited in silence until Matilda came striding towards them.

'Oh, I didn't mean Matilda,' Amari said when she saw the woman.

'You asked for someone I trust.'

'Yes, but I'm sure she has a million things to do.' Amari smiled when Matilda stopped in front of them, no sign of the frustration she'd spoken to him with anywhere. 'Matilda. I'm sorry Kade called you away for this.'

'I work for him,' Matilda said briskly. 'Whatever he needs me to do, I'll do.'

Amari's smile wavered. Kade smiled. 'Thanks, Matilda. We'll be back in less than an hour.'

Amari barely waited until they were around the corner before she hissed, 'An hour? You expect that woman to stand there for an hour?'

'She'll have a table set up within minutes. She's efficient like that.'

'Yeah?'

'Yes.'

'I mean… I guess it's okay if she's productive.' There was a pause. 'But I'm sure having her babysit my child isn't going to make her like me any more.'

'She likes you.'

'She does *not* like me.'

'She's like that with everyone.'

'Not you.'

'I'm her boss.'

'So she said.'

He chuckled. 'You really aren't used to people being curt with you, are you? You prefer being the curt one.'

She angled a look at him. 'I just…' She lingered on that, before rushing into, 'I don't want her to take out her annoyance with me on May.'

Her triumph made him smirk. 'She wouldn't.'

'Good. Then I don't care what she does otherwise.'

When he chuckled again, she glared. He held up his hands, stopped laughing, but didn't bother to hide his smile. They didn't speak much as he led the way to the garden. The few times they did speak, Amari would ask about something on the walls or comment about a piece of art.

'Most of these things were here long before me,' he said, nodding to the guards at the door.

'But when I was young, my father would take me down each passage and tell me about the art.'

'That must have taken a while.'

'It did. But they were some of my favourite memories of growing up.'

'Hmm.' A few seconds later, Amari gasped. 'You've decorated.'

'I was wondering when you'd notice.'

She ran a hand along the garlands that hung from the outside stairs banisters, gently touched the baubles that decorated the wreaths. When they got to the bottom of the staircase, she looked up at the palace, her eyes widening at the lights. They wouldn't go on until later, and he planned to bring both her and May out for that. But even off, they were spectacular. Something about the sheer number.

He liked the Christmas trees that flanked the entrance, too, and the wreath that hung against the usually formal wooden door. Christmas wasn't big in his family. They were usually punctuated by more events, more responsibilities. It meant that he didn't care much about the holiday. Except for this. The decorations, the way his family home looked like something from Father Christmas himself. He particularly loved seeing people's expressions when they saw the decorations. Amari was no different.

Except she was different. He had stopped denying that the moment he'd witnessed her with his parents. It didn't have to mean more than that, he told himself repeatedly, but acknowledging it made it...easier, somehow. Perhaps because it meant he didn't have to concentrate so hard on not thinking about how much she meant to him.

The look on her face now, for example, was much better than the look he'd seen on anyone else's faces when they saw the lights. He couldn't wait to show her the dining hall, once they eventually managed a meal with his parents. Now that his parents had got their questions in—he wanted to speak with them about that, but his mother had been resting after tea, his father out, and he had his own work to do—a meal shouldn't be as contentious as it had been with Amari before.

He was almost looking forward to it.

'When May sees this, she's going to go out of her mind.'

'She likes Christmas, it seems.'

'Loves it,' Amari corrected, still staring up at the palace. 'I don't know what I did to encourage her, since, as you know, I'm a miserable person most days. But somehow, she's managed to drum up a level of excitement for Christmas that I've only seen in children her age.'

'You're doing a good job, then.'

She frowned. 'Why would you say that?'

'Well, if she's excited for Christmas, it means you've allowed her to be. She doesn't have to worry about other things. Money, perhaps. Or whether her parents will be around for Christmas.' He lifted a shoulder. 'I didn't particularly care about Christmas because it came with responsibilities. Engagements.'

'And I didn't care because I was worried about money. And whether my mother would come home for Christmas.' She slanted a look at him. 'If I didn't know any better, I swear you've dug up some information about me.'

'It's not likely I would know information like that, is it?' He neatly skipped over the insinuation. 'I've inferred it. From the little you have said about your mother.'

'Your powers of inference are quite extraordinary.' She was quiet for a few seconds. 'Christmas wasn't a thing when I grew up. My mother wasn't home a lot. When she was, she was always talking about her relationships. It wasn't bad. I had what I needed. For the most part,' she said as an afterthought.

'It doesn't sound like you were afforded the opportunity to be a child.'

'No,' she agreed sadly. 'I was a burden, and I tried not to be.' She exhaled. 'But I've spent too much time resenting my mother for it. I can't change what happened. I can't change her.'

He offered her his arm. After a brief moment of hesitation, she took it. 'Mothers aren't easy, are they?'

She let out a little laugh. 'As someone who has one, and who is one, I think the only answer to that is no, they aren't.' She paused. 'Yours seems a tad challenging, too.'

He snorted. 'She's impossible. I adore her.'

'That much is clear.'

'I am sorry for the way she treated you at tea today.'

'Don't be. I understood. I would do the same thing for my child.'

'You'd try to ascertain someone's intentions towards May?'

'Absolutely.' She squeezed his arm. 'Besides, it's not only you she has to protect. It's the crown, too. I can't imagine how much that must take from her.'

'Too much,' he said. They arrived at the garden, and Kade was saved from spilling out his concerns, his worries. He would have. Told her things he hadn't told anyone before. He shook it off. 'Here we are.'

'What...?' she breathed, but didn't say much else.

Exactly as he intended.

Green stretched as far as the property went, with a large pond that held different-coloured water lilies in the middle. Trees rose up at various heights around the pond, wildflowers of pink and purple bunched at the bottom. A bridge took them over the pond, which was decorated with garlands and lights, too. Though the sky was only just going dark, he'd had the lights turned on for effect. Amari's face told him it had been the right decision.

'This is your backyard?' she asked, voice filled with awe.

'It's one of the official gardens of the kingdom. We open it to the public on certain days of the year. That's why there was such a convoluted journey to get here. We don't want anyone having easy access to the palace.'

'It's amazing.' She went to the edge of the bridge. 'How sturdy is this?'

'Perfectly. It's in use.'

'May I?'

He nodded and she took a step on the bridge. Tentatively, he noted, despite what he'd said. He didn't take offence. This was her personality. She took each step forward carefully. Now that he knew a bit more about her, he understood she was doing it to protect herself. And her child.

He didn't want to keep her from that. He understood the value of protection. He had been protected his entire life, though he'd grown up in the public. There was a force behind his protection. His family, regardless of whether they approved or disapproved of his actions. The communications team, who made sure he was as prepared as he could be when stories went out. There were so many more forms of protection that he hadn't realised.

Amari only had herself.

She had only had herself, for the longest time. And though he wanted to protect her, he wasn't a part of her life. Not in the way that would allow for that to happen. Sure, he was protecting her now, but that was temporary. As soon as things blew over, she would go back home and he would be here, ruling a kingdom.

Suddenly, his plan to kiss her seemed like the stupidest thing.

'Maybe we should head back to the palace,' he said as he followed her. They were almost at the end of the bridge and the moment they got there, she would discover his idiocy.

'Do we have to? I'd love to see what's on the other side.'

'Well, we should probably get ready for dinner,' he hedged. 'Perhaps we should go back and see if May and Matilda are fine.'

She gave him a strange look. 'Are *you* fine?'

'Yes. Yes, of course.'

'I only ask because dinner's in an hour. I checked when I took May up for a nap. And unless they called you, which I don't think they did, since you still sound relatively calm—'

She broke off when she got to the end of the bridge.

He barely resisted his sigh.

CHAPTER TWELVE

AMARI KNEW IT was magical. She would be a fool
not to see it. They were at a palace at Christmas.
At almost every direction, she was reminded that
royalty did Christmas differently from what she'd
grown accustomed to. The magnitude of the decorations, the number of lights, the height of the
Christmas trees. The slides, the elves, the letters
to Father Christmas.

There was also the fact that she felt as if she
had been placed in a fairy tale. The palace was
what she expected to find in those fairy tales. The
garden looked as if it had been designed with royalty in mind. And the prince… Well, the prince
was every bit as delicious as she imagined those
animated princes would be if they were real.

And then there was this.

There was a pathway from where she stood
down until she couldn't see any more. Greenery exploded around them; flowers and leaves
reached through wooden arches above them. It
seemed as if those arches had been built to keep

nature from collapsing on them, and it was beautiful. On either side of the path at regular intervals were wooden benches. Some held gold plaques on them, others had engravings directly on the wood.

If there weren't a small table right in front of them with a bottle of champagne chilling, she would have asked Kade about those plaques and engravings. But there was a bottle of champagne chilling. And there was music playing softly through hidden speakers.

She turned to him. 'Did you do this for me?'

He sighed. 'Would you believe me if I said no?'

'Yes, actually. Your reaction doesn't seem like someone who's done this.'

'You're right. I did do this.' He stared at the table as if it had challenged him to a duel. When he looked at her, his expression was tight. 'I wanted to seduce you into kissing me.'

Her heart hammered against her chest. It had been beating faster from the moment she'd reached the end of the bridge, but this couldn't simply be described as 'beating faster'.

She took an unsteady breath. 'You've…changed your mind?'

'Logic has returned to my mind,' he corrected. He took the champagne from the bucket and poured them both a glass. She took the one he offered, but only held it as he downed his.

'I don't know what I was thinking,' he admitted. 'Kissing you…would complicate matters even more. We haven't spoken about the last time we kissed, and I have no idea what you think about it. All I know is that it upended your life. And then I go do this.' He gestured wildly. 'As if I didn't know that. As if I don't understand that you need to protect yourself and your daughter. As if I didn't want to help protect you.'

'Kade—'

'You deserve more than this life,' he interrupted. 'You deserve your freedom. You deserve—'

'Is that mistletoe?' she asked, when the wind rustled the leaves and something fell to the ground.

Kade let out another sigh. 'Yes.'

'You were planning on seducing me with champagne and mistletoe?'

'Yes.'

She was oddly impressed. 'It's on the floor now though.'

'I can see that,' he answered, his expression pained.

She let it sit for a second, then asked, 'Why? What happened that made you want to seduce me with champagne and mistletoe?'

'You went head to head with my mother.'

'And that…made you want to kiss me?' She

grimaced. 'I understand that we both have issues with our mothers, Kade, but I'll be honest with you—that particular one isn't something I'd like to engage with.'

He gave a quiet laugh. 'No, although that's disgusting and I'm offended you'd say it. No, I meant… You were fierce and strong and honest when you spoke with her. I've seen many other people who've chosen to sacrifice those characteristics with her.'

'Well, she *is* a queen. Perhaps I was foolish for being myself.'

'You could never be foolish for being yourself,' he chided gently. 'And she respects you now because of it.'

'Yeah…well… I suppose…that's fine.'

She put her free hand on her hip, because she had no idea what to do with it. He was flustering her with his compliments. With this entire scene. Yes, there were the champagne and the mistletoe and the garden and the fact that he'd orchestrated the romance and the magic. But it was also his sincerity, the way he looked at her as if he were truly proud of her for being her grumpy old self. It was the way he made her body tingle by simply looking at her. And the way she knew he could make that tingle turn into smoke and fire when he kissed her.

'It's a bad idea,' she said, and not for the first

time when it came to him. 'To kiss you. It's a bad idea.'

'But you're looking at me like that,' he said, his voice deepening as he took in the change on her face.

'And I put down my glass. I'm coming closer.'

'You are.'

'It's the mistletoe,' she said, stopping in front of him. 'We don't generally do the mistletoe thing where I'm from, but it doesn't seem like a good thing to ignore. What if I become cursed?'

'It's a possibility.'

'Hmm.'

She ran a finger over his forehead, down his cheek. She brushed his lips with her thumb, feeling the soft heat of his breath when his lips parted. She touched his neck, the veins that ran there. She pressed her hands lightly to his chest, scraping her nails over his nipples. Her fingers pressed against the ridge of his abs, before hooking into the front of his trousers.

'You feel good,' she whispered.

He smiled. 'There's more to feel.'

She laughed. 'I'm sure there is. How about we just start here though?'

She leaned in until she was inches from his lips.

'I'm happy with that,' he replied, and closed the gap.

The first time he'd kissed her, she had been distracted by the sensations. They had been overwhelming. The taste of him mixed with the wine she'd drunk. The feel of the muscles hard against her body. The heat of his mouth, the expertise of his tongue. All of it had been too much at one time and she'd felt as if she had been sinking beneath the ocean beside them, clinging to him as though he were the only source of air.

This was different. Oh, the sensations were still there. He tasted like champagne now, and of him. Seduction on a Sunday morning. Touches beneath the covers before they were fully awake. He felt warm and hard. A body that could pick her up and toss her over his shoulder. Or press her against a wall and have his way with her without losing a breath. His tongue still tortured her. It slipped over hers, coaxing her to open her mouth wider, to allow him deeper.

Desire flooded her body, touched her breasts, hardened her nipples. It caressed her skin, making every hair stand on end. It teased between her thighs, urging her to press into him, to allow him to soothe and torment at the same time.

But still, it was different.

Perhaps because she felt more present now. The taste, the feeling of him, of her desire, of his, were all there, as if at the tips of her fingers. Power mingled with lust as she tested her presence of mind. As she pulled her mouth from his to press a kiss to his neck, to open her mouth and taste his skin. She grabbed hold of his shirt, tugging until it came free of his trousers, and let her hands feel the heat of his body. She smiled at the tremble, the curse when she brushed her thumbs over his nipples. And she kissed him again as she undid the buttons of his shirt, as she moaned her approval when he helped her.

'Let me see you,' she whispered against his mouth, and with a moan of his own, he stepped back.

She pursed her lips as she took him in. The brown skin that covered muscle, that contained his strength. She didn't care much about a man's body. She thought about it much as she thought of hers. If it allowed her the life she wanted to live, she was pleased with it. But she couldn't deny that this was…enjoyable.

'You look like a prince,' she told him. 'One from a book that couldn't possibly exist.'

'I'm not sure that was a compliment, but I'll say thank you nevertheless.'

'You're such a gentleman.'

'No, I'm not.'

He proved the words by closing the distance between them and picking her up. Her legs automatically went around his waist, then adjusted when he lowered them to one of the benches.

'The garden isn't open to the public today, is it?'

'Of course not,' he told her. 'Do you think I would allow this if there was a chance someone else would see us? I've taken precautions.'

'That's an odd way to phrase it, considering I only plan on kissing you this evening.'

'Oh, no, I didn't mean—' He broke off when she started laughing. 'You'll pay for that.'

'Really? How do you...?'

She trailed off when he kissed her neck.

'I know you meant that as a punishment,' she said, angling to give him better access, 'but it's really not as bad as you think.'

'Stop talking,' he said now, and kissed her.

She fell into it. Into the intimacy of having his tongue tangle with hers. Into the familiarity of it despite that they'd only kissed once before. His hands dug into the flesh at her hips, gripping the fullness, before they moved. She felt the trail along her skin though he didn't have access to it because of her dress. She could only imagine what it would be like if he did have access to her skin. She might have become that trail; a mere path for the pleasure of Kade's hands. She was strangely okay with that.

Slowly, he touched her breasts, testing the fullness of them in his palms. She arched almost without realising. When she did realise, she couldn't bring herself to be upset by it. Here, in the magical garden, she had no shame about her body feeling good. Here, in the magical garden, it was only her and Kade.

She chose to ignore when her mind pointed out that they wouldn't stay in the garden for ever. Instead, she merely focused on his touch.

It was the easiest thing to do.

Something had changed.

It wasn't that they'd made out in the garden he'd spent his childhood running around. Because obviously, that had changed things. Not only between them, but inside him. He couldn't describe how different he felt now that he'd kissed her for more than a few minutes. He didn't know what it meant that the feel of her body in his hands, the taste of her skin against his tongue, felt revelatory.

None of that even touched on how it changed things *between* them. They'd shared private smiles and quiet laughs as they'd righted their clothing after. They'd held hands on their way back to the palace. Amari had insisted on going back to her room alone, which he thought was for the best. She had to focus on May once she got there, and that should be her priority. She didn't need him distracting her with stolen kisses on their way. He didn't want to distract her by pushing her into one of the many dark corners of his home and kissing her all over again.

Yes, it was best that she go to her room by herself.

But now the changes were settling around him in a much less pleasant way. His plan to deal with what had happened in Swell Valley was simple. He'd written a letter to the press explaining that he had taken a short break from duties after a busy year. Because of that short length, they hadn't thought it would be necessary to announce it, as he would be back before any Christmas engagements. While he was there, he'd met a woman he liked and happened to share a kiss with. At this time, he would prefer not to delve into any more than that, especially as the incident had already been a breach of privacy and caused upheaval in both his and the woman's life. He appreciated any respect afforded to this request.

The royal communications team had approved the letter, as had his mother, and though, technically, nothing in the letter was incorrect, it felt disingenuous. Amari wasn't simply 'a woman he liked'. He cared about her. Deeply. That kiss had been a culmination of that. Their kisses today had been an expression of more than attraction. At least for him.

He wanted her at his side when they made the announcement about him being King. His mother wanted to postpone it until after Christmas. She felt that the incident with Amari would cast doubt over his abilities to rule. He didn't agree. At first, he'd thought it was because announcing it now would distract from people's interest in his private life. That would mean Amari could go home, live her life, and move on. Now he wondered if all along it was because he wanted her support. She was the only person he could speak honestly to. He hadn't realised how much he needed that until now.

But that posed another concern. Was he confusing the fact that she was the first person he could talk to with feelings for her? It was feasible. Especially if he threw in the attraction he felt for her. But perhaps that was what relationships were. Feeling a connection with someone he was attracted to. Heaven knew it hadn't ever happened to him before. So maybe he was—

That was what relationships were.

It was a huge step to go from making out with someone to being in a relationship with them. He didn't have to jump to that. He didn't have to have it all figured out.

And that might have been true if he weren't about to become King.

If he were a normal person with normal responsibilities, figuring out whether he wanted to have a relationship with someone would be far simpler. But he wasn't. He'd kissed someone and it had made the front page of every newspaper in the kingdom. How could he explore his feelings, his relationship, in that? Especially when the news that he would be King would intensify the scrutiny he was under?

All of it swirled in his head as he went to dinner that evening. He tried to shake it off, but the looks Amari kept shooting him told him he wasn't quite succeeding. But she didn't get a chance to call him out on it. May had joined them for dinner, and apparently her time in the Christmas station had made the newness of the palace easier to digest. While she wasn't overly chatty—he doubted she was the kind of child who would be—she did say enough to make both Winifred and Deacon laugh in fondness.

He had never thought about his parents' desires for grandchildren. They'd never expressed it, nor had they ever said anything about wanting him to marry. He couldn't believe he hadn't realised that until now. *How* hadn't he realised it until now? He considered his mother's disappointment in him from every angle except this one. Surely she must have wanted him to marry? To have children and continue the line of succession?

But she hadn't said a word about it. And he… he hadn't even thought that she might want him to. Now that he did, he thought she might want him to marry the right person. Someone who could help him rule. Someone who knew the realities of royal life and could raise a child to be aware of those realities, too.

It was another reason Amari wouldn't be right for him. For the family. She hadn't even known he or his kingdom existed before he'd arrived in Swell Valley. She didn't understand royalty and its responsibilities. She was a divorced single mother. Her child was not his child. If he pursued a relationship with her, he couldn't imagine his mother approving of any of these facts. He couldn't imagine the public approving any of these facts.

Did he care?

He wanted to be brave and say no. But he had failed too many times in the past to make such a naïve assertion. Things were becoming way too real with Amari. He was falling for her. He'd caught himself before he was too far gone, but that was over now.

He needed boundaries. And he would have to set them up.

CHAPTER THIRTEEN

AMARI DIDN'T GIVE men a chance to blow hot and cold. She didn't give men a chance at all. She had kept her focus on raising May and running her store ever since things had broken up between her and Hank. No man had interfered with that focus until Kade. And now, he seemed to be the kind of man who blew hot and cold.

He hadn't shown up at her door to guide her down to breakfast that morning. Matilda had. But the woman didn't join her for breakfast, nor did Kade, so she ended up eating with her daughter and the King and Queen of the Kingdom of Daria.

It wasn't awkward, thankfully. Things had settled between tea and dinner the night before. They had settled even more so at the dinner itself. That was the nice thing about being a parent. Rarely did anyone feel so bent out of shape about something that they ignored a kid. Throw in a cute kid—and May was the cutest—and tension barely existed at all.

Kade seemed to be immune to the May effect though. Well, not immune, but it didn't seem to change his obvious tension at dinner the night before. That had nothing to do with May, she'd soon discovered. He'd spoken to her daughter with patience, in a quiet voice that was neither threatening nor overwhelming. May was warming up to him, too. It was all relative with a child like May, but the fact that she was talking to Kade at all? That she had gently pulled Amari to Kade's side so they could sit together at dinner? It was significant.

Amari hated that that significance would blow up in May's face because Kade couldn't talk to her like an adult.

She set it aside. They had the day free, and Matilda had suggested Amari take May down to the beach. It was a great idea since May didn't get to spend much time at the beach, though she loved to swim. Amari simply didn't have the time to take her. Weekdays were out of the question, even in the holidays, because Amari had to work. Weekends, too. Either because Amari had to work or because she had to prepare for work. She tried not to feel bad about it, but she knew it sucked. May deserved to have someone who took her to the beach.

There was no point in lamenting about it, especially on a day Amari *could* take her to the beach.

When they went down to the door, Matilda was waiting with supplies.

'A picnic basket for lunch, sunscreen, and towels. We've already set up a gazebo for you with some beach chairs. You'll be escorted down—' Matilda nodded to a guard hovering nearby '— and find some other guards already there to assist you.'

'Wow, this is…amazing. Thank you.'

'Don't thank me, thank Prince Kade. He arranged for it.'

Of course, Amari thought with a nod at Matilda. There was no way the woman would have done this for her without a push from Kade. And while she wanted to be pleased that he had thought about a way to keep her busy, she suspected that he had done it to keep her busy *away* from him. Something was going on with him. After a fiery make-out session that hadn't been sex, but hadn't been just kisses either, it didn't bode well.

But it was fine. She didn't need him. In fact, it was good. She *didn't* need him. She shouldn't need him. She shouldn't have made out with him, or found him charming, or sweet. Him pulling away actually did them both a favour.

Then why does it feel so damn personal?

She shook her shoulders. Today wasn't about him. It was about her and May and the beach.

And it turned out to be an excellent day. They swam, ate the delicious snacks that had been provided, tanned, built sandcastles, destroyed sandcastles, and laughed. Amari hadn't seen May this happy in a long time. And it hadn't only been at the beach. It had been the day before, too, at that Christmas station.

All of it almost made it okay that she didn't see Kade that day. Or the next, or next, though she and May had full itineraries for both days. On day one, they went to the only theme park on the island. It was prepped for Christmas: elves roamed around, tinsel and garlands and fairy lights decorated storefronts, a Christmas village had been created with Father Christmas distributing Christmas cookies and gifts. May didn't want to get too close to Father Christmas, concerned that he might confuse the gift he gave her with what she'd written in her letters.

Matilda had given Amari the letters May had written Father Christmas at the Christmas station. They were more coherent than Amari expected, but she suspected that was because May had had some elven help. In the first few letters, May had written that she had already sent him her own list, and now, she wanted to send some things through for her mother. On there had been some things Amari had mentioned to no one in particular at home. Body wash, honey, oil. It was cute that May thought Father Christmas could help Amari with her groceries.

The other letters weren't as cute. May asked Father Christmas to send someone to help her mama at the store so she wouldn't always be working. She seemed tired, and May just wanted her mother to be happy. They were sweet requests. Simple.

If only they didn't make Amari feel so guilty.

At least they weren't about May's father. Amari knew she couldn't avoid the topic forever—and she wouldn't—but Amari needed more time to think before she dealt with that. Now, all her time was dedicated to her daughter.

With May's letters in mind, during their second day, when Kade sent them to an aquarium that connected to a rehabilitation centre for penguins, Amari tried to be happy. It wasn't a huge stretch. Pete called her regularly to assure her business was doing well and to ask her about stock and any other things she might need him to order. He also told her the security at her house was working fine and things seemed okay there, too. She didn't have any other responsibilities. Only her kid, who was laughing and happy and didn't seem like a responsibility at all.

The only thing that was slightly off were things with Kade. But that was okay.

Until she saw him the next morning at breakfast and his presence just about kicked her in the gut.

'Hi,' she allowed.

May waved to him. With a pull of Amari's hand, she went to sit beside him and very softly began telling him about what she'd been doing.

Amari merely accepted the tea she'd been offered, before trying to find a distraction. Only then did she realise it was just the three of them.

'Where are your parents?' she asked.

Kade looked up from May. 'My mother wasn't up to a formal breakfast this morning. My father's with her.'

'Is she okay?'

'Fine.' He offered her a nod. 'Just a little fatigued. It's been a busy few days strategising. The announcement's coming up.'

He didn't offer any more than that. She tried to ignore it, but it bothered her. She didn't like that he couldn't talk to her like an adult. She didn't like that he'd run away, or made whatever decision he'd made by himself, without her input.

She was aware that this resentment wasn't entirely because of him. She had some residual anger over Hank. He'd made decisions about their relationship for her, too. He hadn't been willing to try. *He'd* decided and he'd expected her to go along with it.

It wasn't an unreasonable expectation, she

supposed. She had, after all, gone along with it. But she had been a new mother, hormonal, and fighting to be with someone who didn't want to be with her required energy she hadn't had—and wouldn't have for the foreseeable future. She didn't regret it. Hank had walked away from May, not just her. If he could do that so easily when May had been born, there was little doubt in her mind that he could do it later, too. When May was older and capable of feeling that abandonment in a way that would scar her for ever.

The situation was scarily similar to Amari's own life. Her father had left before she got the chance to know him. And perhaps that had been a blessing—she didn't know what it was like to have a father, so she couldn't really miss him—but her mother had been so uninterested in raising her that she'd had fantasies about having a father who cared.

What if May felt that way, too? What if *that* was where her questions came from? What if she saw her mother busy and tired and unhappy and she wondered if having a father would change things? Would May blame Amari in the same way Amari had blamed her mother? Would she wonder what Amari had done to make Hank walk away?

Amari stilled. It wasn't an unusual thought.

She'd had it before. Hell, she'd spent the entire four years of May's life trying to make up for it. But if that thought wasn't going away, she wasn't trying hard enough. If she wasn't as busy, wasn't as tired, wasn't unhappy, surely May wouldn't care about a father?

She couldn't afford to confuse the situation with Kade. May was already getting attached. That could lead to nowhere good when they went back home.

'Amari?'

Amari's head lifted. Kade was looking at her intensely. Her cheeks burned. 'I'm sorry. I got lost in my own thoughts for a second.'

There was the shortest pause. She used it to check on May. Her daughter was picking berries from her plate and stuffing them in her mouth triumphantly.

It made her smile, until Kade said, 'I was wondering if you'd attend an engagement with my parents and me this afternoon?'

'Me?' Amari looked around, as if somewhere she would find a hidden camera. 'Why?'

'We're visiting one of the orphanages in town. It's tradition to go there, do some activities with them, then have lunch and hand out gifts.'

'I still… Well, wouldn't it be better if I weren't with you?' She dropped her head, not believing Kade didn't see the flaw in his plan. 'I imagine any event where you and I are together will garner the kind of attention you don't want.'

'This is different,' Kade said smoothly. 'We only invite a small group of reporters, all from publications we trust. Our instructions this time around will be to picture only official members of the royal family. We'll allow them to mention you were there—not by name, of course—because it might change the public's perception of you.'

'You mean as someone other than the woman who seduced the prince?'

Kade's lips pursed. 'Yes.'

If he got upset by her describing seduction, how did he expect her to feel about him actually seducing her? That she'd allowed him to, and that he seemed to regret it?

'I think it's a bad idea,' Amari said. 'If I'm there and they mention it, it will seem as if we're dating, and we're not,' she added flatly, as if he needed the clarification.

Maybe the clarification was for her.

'The kingdom already knows you're here.' Kade's face was impassive. He was being the Polite Prince again.

'What does that mean, exactly?'

'Nothing.'

'No, it means something. It must mean something or you wouldn't have come up with this.'

Now, Kade looked pained. 'I think… It might change the public's mind about you being here.'

Ah, so that was it. He wanted to make her more palatable. If she helped with a charity event, she would seem less like an evil seductress. But what she couldn't figure out was why. Why did it matter to Kade what his kingdom thought of her?

Or was it because their opinion of her was a reflection of their opinion of him?

'What do you want me to do?' she asked quietly, ignoring the question her inner voice was asking *her*.

Why does his kingdom's opinion of him matter to you?

Something akin to gratitude fluttered in Kade's eyes. It was a pity she didn't want it.

'I thought it would be good to have you lead them in some crafts. It doesn't have to be anything fancy. A simple activity would do.'

'And you believe this will change people's opinions of me?'

'I do.'

'And what about you?'

He was quiet for a moment. 'I'm not sure what you mean.'

'Of course you do,' Amari replied. 'You've come up with this plan to redeem my image, although really it's your image.' She paused. 'I know it doesn't matter what your kingdom thinks of me. When I leave, no one will even remember me. But it matters that the woman you kissed on a beach—currently living in the palace—hasn't manoeuvred her way into a first-class holiday or life.'

She was looking at May by the end of it, speaking as calmly as she could so May wouldn't pick up her tension. She knew it might be futile. Children were good at picking up undercurrents, and she couldn't control those other than her own. But she would try.

She smiled when May looked up at her, and took a bite of the pancake May offered. She didn't look up until she was done chewing. Kade was staring at her with something fierce shining in his eyes. She wanted to say it was respect, and perhaps it was, but it didn't matter.

'I'll do it,' she told him. 'I have no desire to sabotage your reputation, or the reputation of your family.' Her own breakfast was put in front of her and she picked up her utensils. 'Now— shall I speak to Matilda about the details, or do you already have those for me?'

CHAPTER FOURTEEN

AMARI WAS FIRE. Passion. Strength. Kade knew it, of course, so he wasn't sure why he was surprised.

Perhaps he had forgotten. He'd certainly tried to. He'd spent three days avoiding her. Keeping both of them busy separately so he wouldn't think about her and she wouldn't think about him. Her icy look that morning at breakfast told her he might not have succeeded. She had clearly thought about him—and not in good ways.

It was for the best. It would be harder to forget her and the effect she had on him if she still wanted him. After what she had said that morning, he saw he'd made that decision for her. Just as he'd made the decision about the orphanage visit. The shame he felt told him he needed to apologise. But something deeper told him that, too. Not only for making decisions for her, but for avoiding her.

And he had to do it all without mentioning that

her fire, passion and strength were exactly why she was such trouble for him.

He found her in the playroom he'd arranged for May. May was currently focusing hard on colouring in. Amari was sitting in the corner near the window, staring out of it. From there, he knew she could see the garden. Was she thinking about what they'd done in there? Was she regretting it? Reliving it?

He shook his head. 'Amari.'

Both she and May looked over. May gave him a shy smile that filled his heart, but she continued colouring. Amari merely stared at him. After a few seconds, she nodded her head. He approached with caution.

'Matilda said the kids at the orphanage are around May's age,' she said when he sat down. She didn't look at him. 'We came up with some great ideas. She's working on one of them. Making Christmas decorations.'

'They'll love it.'

'Your mother thought so, too. I ran the idea by her during tea earlier.'

Neither of them said anything after that for a bit. Kade exhaled. Then he inhaled and said, 'I'm sorry.'

'For what?'

It was just like her to not allow him to be vague. But she deserved the clarity.

'I should have involved you when I came up with this plan.'

'Why?' she asked, pulling her knees up to under her chin. She was looking at him now, and somehow the position made her look so vulnerable, his heart ached. 'You're used to making decisions for others. That's how you run a kingdom, isn't it?'

'It's not supposed to be.' He straightened his shirt sleeves. 'We have a parliament we rule alongside. Whenever there are decisions to be made, we make them with the representatives our people have voted in.'

'Oh.' There was a beat. 'So you just make them for me, then.'

'You don't understand how many things come into play with something like this.'

'Maybe not,' she said evenly, 'but I am both emotionally and intellectually capable. If you'd talked to me about the idea—*talked*, not told—I would have easily agreed. I might have even contributed something valuable. But you didn't give me that opportunity.'

'You're right.' He shook his head. He was getting into an argument for no other reason than his pride. He'd already admitted he needed to apologise. He had already apologised. And now he was defending his actions. 'I'm sorry. This situation is…difficult for me. I want to protect you.'

'Protecting me isn't robbing me of my agency. It's allowing me to choose, to be a part of something, especially when it pertains to me and my actions.' She frowned. 'And you're not protecting me. You're protecting yourself.'

'I know. I know.'

'And I'm not only talking about this thing with the orphanage.'

He cast an eye towards May. She wasn't paying attention to them, but was engrossed in colouring in a Christmas star for a tree.

'That's different.'

'How?'

'It's… There's no future with us.'

'I know that,' she snapped. She looked at May, too. Lowered her voice. 'Do you think I don't understand the complexities of any relationship with you? I do. Which is why I'm not asking for a relationship. A couple of kisses don't mean I want a relationship.'

'They weren't only a couple of kisses,' he told her, as if he needed to defend what they'd shared.

She snorted. 'Oh, so now there's more to it? Didn't you pretend it didn't happen for three days?'

'I…'

'Yeah,' she said when he trailed off. 'There's no real excuse for that.'

'I was protecting myself.'

They were useless words. Empty words. But still, she nodded.

'I understand that. I do. But I wasn't the one who created the perfect magical opportunity to make out outside my home. I didn't pursue you in any way, or seduce you. I didn't ask you for anything more than you were willing to give, and those opportunities you created, that seduction… That made me think you were a willing participant.'

'I…was.'

'Okay, you were. You're not any more. That's perfectly okay. Just don't…' She exhaled and lowered her feet to the floor. 'Look, I've been here before, okay? Deeper in, because I was married to him and had a kid with him. He decided things weren't working for him any more and I had to accept that. And I did. But I still resent him. I resent him because he didn't give me any say. I resent him because my kid doesn't have a father, and likely never will, because he decided he didn't want to be one.'

'That's why he left?'

She snorted lightly. 'He didn't like the responsibility of a newborn. Six months in, when things were the toughest, he decided life was easier without a child. It is,' she acknowledged, 'but that's something you should talk about before you get married. It's a decision you make together. It's not something you discover after you get your wife pregnant and make her think she's lucky because she has you and all your support.'

'He sounds like a jerk.'

'Yeah?' She clucked her tongue. 'That situation was worse than this, no doubt, but I guarantee you when I go home and tell Lydia about all this, she's going to say the same thing about you.'

He stared at first, then he chuckled. 'You're right.'

'I know.'

'I'm sorry.' He took a beat. 'That your husband wasn't good to you either.'

She heaved out a sigh. 'I wish I could tell you that I'm over it, but I'm not. Him and my mom—' She shook her head. 'They hurt me, and I carry that with me all the time.' She looked at him. 'So when you do something like this, it takes me back to the people in my life who didn't consider me. They only thought about themselves. I get that that's on me, I do, but…'

'It's not only on you. Not if…'

He was the one to trail off now. Because he had been about to say, 'Not if we're in a relationship,' and clearly, they weren't. But he cared about her. He cared about not hurting her, and he had been selfish for not even considering it before.

'It's not only on you,' he said again, more firmly. 'I have things that trigger me, too. The reason I tried not to see you for three days is… You mean something to me. I don't know what, and I thought I should. This isn't a world you bring someone into when you're not sure about how you feel. And I was convinced—'

He broke off, ashamed of what he had thought. How could he tell her he was convinced she wasn't right for him? He didn't care about her past for himself. He only thought his family would care. His kingdom. That was a shameful thing to admit out loud.

Luckily, she didn't push him. She merely nodded and stared out of the window again.

'I'm not sure either,' she said eventually. 'And I should know, too. My responsibility might not be a kingdom, but it's as important to me as your kingdom is to you.'

She looked at May. When her gaze rested back on him, she nodded. 'I understand why you don't want to pursue this. And I…agree. You have my permission to avoid me.'

'Amari—'

'No, Kade, you're right. This isn't…we can't do this. There's too much at stake. Especially when we don't even know what this is.'

Why did it feel so devastating? It was the exact same conclusion that he had come to. But hearing it from her…it felt final. And his heart wasn't entirely ready to handle that.

Did that matter, though?

He stood. 'So—we're okay?'

'We're deciding this together. That's all I wanted.' She stood with him. 'We're okay.'

They were standing close enough that he could feel the heat coming off her body. His body immediately responded. Fingers itched to touch; skin prickled for her touch; his heart pounded so hard it felt as if it wanted to jump out of his chest into hers.

Not touching her felt like a tragedy. All of it did.

Something niggled at his brain, his heart, but he ignored it. It didn't matter. The only thing that mattered was that he made his mother and kingdom proud.

He didn't examine why that felt like a lie.

CHAPTER FIFTEEN

THE TRIP TO the orphanage once again proved Kade had underestimated Amari. He was well aware it reflected poorly on him, and his only consolation was that he would try to do better. He was also immeasurably proud of Amari. She displayed the kind of behaviour he could only describe as grace. It wasn't a term he used often. In fact, it was only a term he used for his mother.

But it suited Amari. Perhaps even more than it did his mother.

She worked with the children easily, not showing the discomfort he usually saw when adults were around kids. She was a mother, which he supposed helped, but he didn't think motherhood had changed her all that much. He could easily see her respond in the same way even if she weren't a mother. She gave them affection, showed them patience, enthusiasm when they called her to show off the tiniest thing. Not once did she look annoyed or frustrated by it, even when a young boy crawled into her lap and clung to her without showing any desire to let go.

May had come with them, and at that, she'd given the boy a long look. But her mother winked at her, and something about it must have made May realise her mother cuddling another child didn't rob her of anything. It was the only explanation he could come up with as to why she merely went back to the task at hand.

The staff were impressed. He didn't have to see the smiles of approval they sent his way to know. They murmured, actually vibrated, as they talked about her. He wanted to tell them it was impolite. It was obvious they were talking about Amari. But she didn't seem to care. She ignored the whispers. Returned the smiles. When she met his eyes, she rolled her own slightly, but seconds later she was speaking to a child and if anyone had seen it, they would doubt they had.

As Amari handled the crafts with the children, he and his parents spoke with some of the beneficiaries of the orphanage. It was more of the usual. Gratitude for their generosity. Patience when they expressed concerns or plans. Kade tried to engage as much as he could, but his eyes kept going back to Amari.

Why was he so surprised she was good at this?

'You're staring,' his mother said under her breath as she lowered into a chair. She seemed tired, but it wasn't unusual for an event to make her feel that way. Besides, they were coming up to the announcement of her abdication, and he couldn't imagine that helped her sleep.

'It's involuntary,' he admitted.

'She is rather magnificent.'

He turned to his mother. 'What?'

'You heard me. Here, take a seat,' she ordered, pointing to one. 'It will seem less suspicious that I'm sitting if you do, too.'

He obeyed, giving his father a nod when Deacon caught his eye. He would stay with his mother while Deacon drew the attention of anyone who might question it. His father didn't like being social, but he would do anything for his wife. It also helped that they were preparing the gifts around Kade and his mother, and it seemed as though they were merely supervising.

'I heard you,' Kade said. 'I suppose I was wondering if you'd really said it or if I was making it up.'

'You can be so dramatic,' Winifred said with a shake of her head.

He smiled. 'Where do you think I get that from?'

She slanted him a look, but didn't address the comment. 'I said it because I believe it. She's surpassed my expectations.'

'What were those expectations?'

'Of a divorced single mother?' She let the question linger for a moment. 'Nothing that wasn't merely prejudice on my part. If I thought she would care, I'd apologise.'

'I don't think she does care.'

'That much is clear. If she cared about what I think, she wouldn't have said any of what she said to me in this last week.'

He smiled. 'I'm pleased she did. What?' he asked when his mother gave him a shrewd look. 'No one is assertive with you. They tend to be too scared.'

'Even you?'

'Especially me.'

His mother was silent for a while. 'In the weeks since you've known her, you've been more assertive and decisive. The decision to bring her here was bold.'

He didn't know how to respond, so he remained quiet.

'I don't think she's changed you,' his mother continued, musing more than anything else. 'But I think she's allowed you to step into yourself. Perhaps that's because she's so unapologetically herself, or because you love her, and thus want to protect her. Either way, I'm pleased it's happened now.' She reached out to take his hand. 'It's all I've ever wanted for you, Kade.'

His silence now wasn't because he couldn't

form an answer, but because he was stunned. There were so many parts to this. The fact that his mother approved of Amari, though he'd believed she wouldn't. His mother wanting him to be himself when he'd spent a lifetime believing the opposite. She supported him in a way he hadn't believed possible.

Through all of it, he could only say one thing, 'I don't love Amari.'

'Of course you don't, dear.' His mother patted his hand. 'You've merely stepped into the man I've always believed you could be because of a kiss.' She laughed. 'It must have been some kiss.'

She laughed again.

She was laughing at *him*.

'I've spent my life thinking you didn't believe I could do this job.' His voice was hard.

'I never once thought you couldn't do this job. But I didn't believe you wanted to do this job. You were never interested in the work, Kade. You were more interested in pleasing me. And while I can't fault you for it—I'm your mother and it made me quite happy that you wanted to please me—it's distracted you from your potential.'

'My…? Mother, this is a lot.'

'We can discuss it later,' she said. 'With more privacy, too.' She paused, then dropped his hand and turned to look at him. 'I will say this, as you seem to need to hear it. I've always wanted you to be yourself, Kade. I'd hoped you'd come to the conclusion long before I had to say it.'

'What about all those mistakes I made? What about the disappointment you felt?'

'The mistakes came because you were trying to be like me. I wanted you to be yourself, and I was disappointed that you didn't believe you could be.'

His heart was racing, and it wasn't entirely comfortable. Neither were his thoughts. He knew he needed time to process, and that now, at an event, wasn't the best time to do so.

But he couldn't help but think about how he'd misinterpreted things. How he'd made up this narrative because he was so convinced that he knew his mother, he didn't give her the chance to surprise him.

Because you didn't ever ask her.

Amari had asked him that several times. *'Has your mother ever said she's disappointed in you?'* Each time he'd said no, but dismissed it because he was so sure she was. He'd spent a lifetime believing it, after all. Amari posing a simple question hadn't been enough to undermine that belief. Only this conversation had.

Which made him think about something else Amari had said. About how he made decisions for them, for her. He'd done the same thing with his mother. He'd decided she was disappointed in him. He'd decided he wasn't enough. He'd decided not to engage with his mother about it, or talk to her about what she thought he was doing wrong.

He'd decided all these things without ever once speaking openly with his mother. If he had, it would have saved him so much heartache. If he had known his mother didn't care about him being her, only himself, he would have spent the last years growing into who he could be as King. He wouldn't have messed up trying to be who he thought his mother wanted him to be.

He'd also decided that his mother wouldn't approve of Amari. That he needed to have the right kind of wife for his family and kingdom. But his mother didn't care about that. She cared that Amari was a woman of integrity. She had reflected on her prejudices and faced her mistakes. That was the woman, the ruler, his mother was.

And he had spent a lifetime casting his own fears and opinions onto her.

What the hell did that say about him?

Amari liked helping those children more than she'd expected she would. Some of that was because she hadn't exactly known what *to* expect. In her mind, she had pictured the press clamouring to get pictures of the harlot who had tempted their prince into sin, despite what Kade had told her about which press would be there. She had thought people would judge her, and treat her poorly.

None of that had happened. And once she'd realised it wouldn't, she'd allowed herself to relax. She'd enjoyed it. Speaking with the children. Helping them, watching May interact with them. She imagined that this was what it would be like to volunteer at May's school. She had never had the opportunity to; she was always too busy working. Now, she felt as if she'd missed something valuable. May around children was a delight, and she wished...

Well, she wished she could be in her daughter's life more. Because it wasn't *this* that was delightful. It was spending time with May. It was watching her engage with the world and navigate new experiences. And yes, doing something this meaningful with her somehow felt more significant, but Amari wasn't foolish enough to believe she wouldn't feel the exact same way in other circumstances. This time in Daria had taught her what she had lost with May. And made her wonder if she was willing to keep losing it.

'Are you okay?' Kade asked on the way home. It was only the three of them in the car. His parents had taken their own. 'You've been quiet.'

'As have you,' she countered, because she

wasn't in the mood to talk about it. 'I saw you and your mother having an intense conversation. Are *you* okay?'

He looked out of the window before he replied. Amari couldn't help but notice how beautiful his kingdom was. Rolling green hills, bodies of water, flowers everywhere… Somehow, Daria had been blessed with the most beautiful of what nature had to offer. She would miss the simplicity of it when she went home.

Home.

Strange, she hadn't thought about it since they'd arrived. Stranger yet, she hadn't missed it since they'd arrived. She had what she needed with her. Why had it taken her such a long time to see it?

Because you're distracted.

'I am,' Kade replied, interrupting her thoughts, yet somehow proving them as well. 'We had… The conversation was good. It's showed me that a lot of my preconceived ideas were created based on my own fears.'

'That's a deep thing to say.'

He looked at her with a half-smile. 'I'm still working on it, but I've managed to come to that conclusion.'

'It can't have been easy,' she said, studying his face.

'It's not.'

'But it's worth it.' She shrugged at his furrowed brows. 'Whenever you realise your actions come from a place of fear instead of something positive, it propels you in the direction of something positive.'

She ran her hand over May's head. Her little girl was sleeping on her lap. It had been an exhausting day. The simple comfort of it filled her heart.

'Take this, for example. I was so scared of becoming like my mother...' She trailed off when her eyes burned. Looked out of the window. 'I'm trying to be a better mother to May. That fear turned into something beautiful.'

Has it?

She bit her lip. The beauty of raising May hadn't erased any of her fears about being her mother. And it hadn't entirely changed her either. She was still making decisions that reminded her of her mother. She wasn't putting May first. That entailed protecting May and loving her. It entailed giving May the mother she wanted; a mother who wasn't tired and busy. A mother who was happy.

She shook her head. 'But then, what do I know?'

'Not enough, if you're still comparing yourself to your mother.'

She snorted. 'You don't know my mother.

She…she's self-centred. Which isn't necessarily a bad thing.'

'Unless you're a parent.'

'Yes.'

They were quiet for a bit.

'She's not a bad person,' she continued softly, loyalty compelling her. 'She agreed not to sell any stories about me to the papers. That's something.'

He nodded. 'I suppose you don't have to be a bad person to be a bad mother.'

Why did it feel as if he was describing her?

But no, she wasn't a bad mother.

Was she?

'What were your fears?' she asked, desperate to get out of her head.

'You're deflecting.'

'Obviously.'

He looked to the sky, as if asking for strength, though his lips twitched. 'I've told you my mother's disappointed in me because I can't rule as she does.'

'You have.'

'As it happens, she's been disappointed in me because I've tried.' The disbelief on his face made her want to reach out. A stronger emotion inside her kept her from doing so. 'She's spent my entire life waiting for me to do *my* best. Not what I think she thinks is my best, but *mine*. She wanted me to be me, and I spent a lifetime trying to be her.'

Amari opened her mouth, but she didn't think what she wanted to say would be welcomed.

'What?' he asked.

'What do you mean?'

'You don't have to feign ignorance. Especially when your face is the most expressive I've seen.'

'I might not have to feign ignorance, but I can check whether you truly want to hear what I'm going to say since it's probably going to sound snarky.'

'And when has that ever stopped you.'

'Hey—I'm trying over here.'

He angled his head. 'Apologies. Would you tell me? I'd like to know.'

She gave him a beat to change his mind. And silently thanked him for drawing her out of her own problems.

'Okay, this is what I've been thinking since you told me your mom's disappointed in you. You're great. Genuinely great. You're kind and thoughtful. You carry yourself in a way I'd expect a prince to, though I'm not completely sure I'm the best judge. You're smart, have a big heart, and you do well under pressure. Working in my store put you under pressure—you and I both know it,' she added to clarify. 'You don't like not knowing things, but you didn't once snap, or make me feel like it was my fault, or do something ridiculous. You listened. You tried your best. I couldn't understand how your mother wouldn't see that in you. I mean, she's known you your entire life and I've known you for weeks.'

'I... I...'

When he kept stammering, this prince who was smooth and rarely speechless, she smiled. 'I know it's hard to get out of your own head. But it's true. This is who you are: a king. And the fact that you couldn't see that only proves how much you deserve to be King. Anyone who wants to do better for their loved ones, for their people? Yeah, they deserve to rule a kingdom.' She lifted a shoulder at his stare. 'All this kingdom can ask for is someone who wants to do their best.' She looked back down at May. 'All anyone can ask for is someone who does their best.'

For a long while, they drove in silence. Amari didn't mind. It gave her the opportunity to get her thoughts in order. She needed to change her life, and she knew that if she didn't do it when she got back, she would get sucked back into routine and it would be harder. This was already going to be the hardest thing she had done.

'Amari.'

The softness of Kade's voice sank into her heart before she saw his expression. It stole her breath even though she didn't allow herself to think about what she was seeing there.

'You're a good mother.'

She swallowed. 'Yeah. Yeah, I know.'

'No, you don't. I can see you're judging yourself. I don't know what the basis of it is, but I know that it's not deserved. You're doing your best. It's all she can ask for, as you just said.'

'Except I'm not,' she replied. 'I'm using motherhood to fight my own demons and she deserves…she deserves more.'

His gaze was intense. 'And you'll give her more.'

'I'm going to try.'

'And that means you're a good mother.'

She blew out a breath, but offered him a smile. 'Thank you.'

'Don't thank me. Believe it.'

If only it were that easy.

CHAPTER SIXTEEN

THE DAYS PASSED in a blur after that first charity event. Amari hadn't expected it to be a first, but Queen Winifred had asked Amari to assist her with some of her festive charity obligations. Amari couldn't say no. Especially when the Queen had made the request because she was 'feeling weak'. She had said those words looking both shrewd and strong, but Amari could hardly point that out.

Queen Winifred was probably counting on that.

The upside was that the work was inspiring. All the events were for charities supporting children. Some assisted those who'd experienced some form of violence by teaching them how to defend themselves. Others supported those without one or both parental figures. Some fed children at foster homes; took children off the street; worked to improve conditions in orphanages.

She didn't know why Queen Winifred had chosen her to help with these charities specifically.

Was it because Amari had her own child? Or had she simply done a good job at the orphanage? It certainly couldn't be because the Queen knew Amari felt fulfilled by it. She wasn't even doing that much, merely talking to the children and the staff, helping out where she was needed, yet her heart was filled by it. It felt like…like purpose. She hadn't experienced that in a long time. Not since May was born. Not even with her store.

If she spent too long thinking about that, loyalty speared a lance through her chest and she leaked guilt. Because her store *did* give her purpose. It did. She had built it from the ground up. It belonged to her and would some day belong to May. It provided for them. It meant something to them. To the community.

But it also kept her busy. It kept her from spending time with May. It caused anxiety and fear, neither of which allowed her to be the mother she wanted to be.

The guilt ate at her.

She thought talking about it might make things better, but the only person she wanted to talk to was Kade. And things with him were…complicated. He accompanied them to the charity events—another reason Amari was convinced the Queen didn't need her—and he was splendid.

She had only seen him in his official capacity once before, at the orphanage, but she could tell he was different now. He wasn't as tense any more. He didn't seem to be bracing for something no one else could see. And witnessing him being himself, witnessing everyone see what she saw in him, was special. It did something to her heart. Just as seeing him with May did.

Somehow, they always found their way to one another. They didn't talk much, but it didn't seem to matter to either of them. They looked for each other in a room. May would take his hand; his would swallow hers. And he didn't seem to care one bit that they got curious glances.

Amari wondered if *she* should care. Did it matter that there had already been insinuations on gossip sites about who May was? About what she meant to Kade? There were stories about Amari, too, though she didn't waste her time thinking about those. No, May was her main concern. Except May wasn't hurt by the insinuations. Neither was Amari. But Kade must have been.

Of course, no official media outlet had run with the stories. Kade's case against the newspaper who had taken the picture of them kissing on the beach was still ongoing; no one seemed willing to take the chance that they'd be next. They had even signed legal documents that prevented them from mentioning or taking pictures of her and May at any of the events. Amari could only

imagine what Kade had offered them in return.
And yet he didn't seem unhappy or worried.

The only time she saw those emotions was
when she caught him looking at her.

That mainly happened at the events, as she and
Kade barely spoke then. But after, they always
seemed to find one another. Sometimes it was in
the afternoon; other times, the evening. But every
day they found moments to spend together. They
either supervised May as she played, or went for
a walk after May went to bed. And they talked.
About superficial things, mostly. They were careful to stay away from talks of family, of responsibility, of them.

But still, their talks didn't feel superficial.
They felt special, as if she were pushing open a
door that had been stuck for a long time, letting
long-overdue air into a stuffy room.

Somehow, the talking led to handholding. To
lingering stares and kisses on the cheek. She ignored the significance of it, of any of it, because
there was no point in acknowledging it. Nothing
had changed. He was still going to be King; she
was still May's mother. They had their responsibilities. Talking, handholding, lingering stares
and kisses didn't matter.

Even if teasing him about wanting to knit; feeling his skin as she held his hand; falling into the

liquid depths of his eyes; brushing her lips to his cheek made her day.

'What's this?' she said to no one, really, when she reached the door of her room and an envelope was stuck to it. They had just come back from a walk, where she'd made the mistake of mentioning ice cream. Ignoring May's insistence that they needed ice cream *now*, she opened the envelope.

Please be ready at two p.m.
Matilda

That was all.

Frowning, Amari looked at her watch. It was one-thirty. She had thirty minutes to get ready, and she had no real idea what that meant. She shuffled May into the room, distracting her with TV, and took a shower. After, she stared at the closet. Most of the clothes she'd been wearing recently had come from Matilda.

'We need you to look a certain way,' the woman had said, before telling her exactly which outfit to wear to which event. Since there had been no instructions this time around, Amari chose something from her own clothing. A simple black dress that could be dressed up or down depending on the occasion. She decided on down since she probably wouldn't have been given the chance to decide for herself if she needed to dress up.

'Good, you're ready,' Matilda said when Amari opened the door to her knock precisely at two.

'Is this okay?'

'It's fine. I'm only taking you shopping.'

'Oh.' She frowned. 'Is that necessary? The sizes you've got for me have been fine so far.'

'It's easy to pick something for obligations,' Matilda said crisply. 'This is for the ball tomorrow night.'

'Tomorrow...' she trailed off.

They were announcing Queen Winifred's abdication at the ball the following night. They would also be announcing Kade's coronation would take place a few days into the new year. It was a big deal.

'I didn't think I would be going.'

'Both the Queen and Prince Kade have indicated their desire to have you and May present.'

'May—'

'Are we going to the ball, Mama?'

May perked up from where she sat on the bed. Amari narrowed her eyes. She hadn't realised May had been listening.

'No, honey. We're just—'

'It's not advised to ignore an invitation from royalty,' Matilda said blandly.

'Hmm.'

'Mama, we should do it. We can get pretty dresses.'

'Yes,' Matilda said. 'In fact, we're doing that right now.'

May squealed with happiness. Amari gave Matilda a stern look. 'Don't think I don't know I've just been manipulated.'

For the first time since Amari met Matilda, the woman smiled.

Kade couldn't quite describe what it was like walking into that room and seeing Amari in a ball gown. He should have waited until the following night to see her in the full outfit, but he wanted to make sure that she was okay. He also didn't know what the night would look like. He did know most of the attention would be on him, and that his couldn't be consumed by a woman he wasn't supposed to be in love with because she looked gorgeous in a gown.

The fact that she stole his attention completely from the moment he saw her in the gown told him it was good he hadn't waited.

The fact that he was absolutely in love with her seemed almost irrelevant in light of that.

'I asked them to put you in red because it reminded me of that day at the beach,' he said into the room.

Amari whirled around, causing the skirt of her dress to spin around her as if she were a fairy-tale princess. He didn't care for the fairy-tale part, but he wanted her to be a princess. Or a queen. The title suited her better anyway.

Kade.

Right. He needed to rein in his fantasies until after the ball. That had to be his main priority.

But it was just so damn easy to imagine her in his life.

Spending the weeks with her in his kingdom had been amazing. And the last week… Well, that had been something else entirely. She handled each event she attended with grace and poise. It was almost as if she'd been born for it. It was significant, considering she hadn't had any preparation, but that was part of the charm. She spoke with people honestly, relating to them in ways he knew he never could.

His mother's words at the first charity event had stuck with him. Perhaps that was why, when he realised he was in love with her, he wasn't entirely surprised. His feelings for her didn't feel taboo any more either. She would be good for the kingdom. And his mother approved. Hell, she was fond of Amari and May in ways he had never thought possible.

Which was why, after the ball, he was going to propose.

'You're biased,' Amari said, smoothing down the front of her dress. There was no reason for the action to draw his attention to her chest, but it happened anyway. The sweetheart neckline showed off the smooth lines of her clavicle, the expanse of her golden-brown shoulders, the curve of her cleavage.

He forced his eyes up. 'I am. It was a good day.'

'I had to move to a kingdom I never knew existed because of that day,' she chided, but the edges of her mouth pulled up.

'You're happy here though, aren't you?'

It was a loaded question, deliberately so. He wanted to know what his chances were. She smiled—a private, intimate smile that made him want to chase the designer out of the room so only he could see it. So only he could witness the moment he realised his chances were *good*.

'I have been.' Her eyes twinkled, warming his insides. 'This has been the best Christmas May and I have had. Right, sweetheart?'

Amari winked at him. For a second, he didn't know why. Then she moved, stepping to the side to reveal a miniature version of her.

May had an almost identical dress on to Amari, though hers went higher up at the neck. She looked at him shyly, but expectantly. He hid his smile as he walked to the front of her, before dropping to his knees.

'You, darling May, look like a princess.'

May beamed. 'I look like Mama.'

'Yes,' he agreed. 'And your mother looks like a princess, too.'

He looked at Amari as he said it, hoping she would see through the words to his meaning. He wanted her to be his princess. His queen. He wanted her to rule beside him. She made him a better person. She made him a better king—she had done long before he was even supposed to be King. What effect wouldn't she have once he was?

For a moment, it felt as if she did see his true meaning. Their eyes held, electricity sparked. He remembered what it felt like to have her body against his, the softness of her lips, the teasing of her tongue. It hadn't happened in much too long, but he was a patient man. He would experience it again.

Hopefully, for a lifetime.

She looked away and May started speaking to him as the designer drew Amari to the side, putting pins into the dress and murmuring. The moment was over.

He tried not to project any meaning onto it.

CHAPTER SEVENTEEN

THE MOMENT AMARI walked into the ballroom, she knew she would remember the experience for ever.

Perhaps it would be for a simple reason, like the décor. It was spectacular: the crystals glistening from the roof that looked like ice and snow; the lights dangling down the walls, casting the room with a warm glow. Or perhaps the reason would be more significant. The joy in May's eyes as she took in the Christmas tree, the presents beneath it, the throne that was regal and gold and breathtaking...

Then, of course, there was the way Kade looked at her when he noticed her in the room.

Amari felt it before she saw it. It hit her between her shoulders and she turned, catching his eyes immediately. The rise in her temperature came from a deep, intimate place inside her. Her skin felt sticky even as it turned into gooseflesh as he stared and stared, much as she had the first time she had seen him.

He gave her an almost imperceptible nod an endless amount of time later, just as May pulled at her hand. Amari looked down for a second, then back up, but Kade's attention was already elsewhere and her daughter was dragging her to a Christmas tree.

And that was when the magic stopped.

Because it quickly become obvious that May was the only child there. Amari had assumed, because Kade and his parents had invited them, that that wouldn't be the case. She had assumed they would know people already saw them as outsiders. She had assumed the royal family would protect her and May and not give people any more reason to stare. But apparently that had been too much to hope for.

People *did* stare at them. And they whispered, or ignored them entirely. She hadn't anticipated how awful it would make her feel. She had known that she would only know Kade and his parents there, and that they wouldn't have time to talk with her, but she'd thought she could mingle. She had, at the charity events. She had done fine in those circles. But she was beginning to realise it was because she was like the people at those charity events; it wasn't because she was like Kade.

It twisted inside her. Became an ugly, sharp weapon that pierced into hopes and dreams she hadn't given herself a chance to entertain. Hopes and dreams she'd thought she had discarded when she realised who Kade was.

And yet here she was, devastated because it was clear she didn't fit into his life. Because it was clear that in the last two weeks they had been living in a reality that could never exist.

And she was angry. Angry at Kade for bringing her here and making her believe it could exist. For inviting her to a ball she had no business being at.

It didn't take a genius to know she was really angry at herself. Because once again, she had put her own desires above her daughter's. And once again, it hadn't worked out.

So when May began to complain, to pull at her dress, Amari immediately picked her up. Her heart ached when May hid her face in Amari's shoulder, a clear sign that she had felt the tension in the room, too.

She made the decision quickly: she wasn't staying. She would send Kade an apology for not making it through the announcement or the dinner, but she *couldn't* stay. Even though she wanted to. She wanted to make those people uncomfortable by staring back, whispering back, making them feel as small as they intended on making her feel. But she couldn't do it alone—and she was. Utterly alone. More importantly, trying to prove a point wasn't the best thing for May.

She owed her daughter her best. Even if she kept failing, she still needed to try.

May was quiet when they reached the room, and Amari got her into bed without much of a fuss. She wanted to call down for dinner, but she worried with the event happening that she would be asking for too much. Since she refused to let her daughter go hungry for the night, she called Matilda. She felt as if the woman would have an easier time securing food without being an inconvenience.

The food arrived less than twenty minutes later. They ate, Amari sang May to sleep, and, when she finally succeeded, Amari put off all the lights. She had taken off her dress to convince May to do the same, and wore one of her own. But she hadn't taken off her make-up or undone her hair, and she couldn't bring herself to do either. Instead, she curled up around May, caressing her forehead and silently promising her she would never put her in this position again.

When the knock came hours later, Amari still hadn't fallen asleep. She had expected it, though she only knew that when it was already there. She tiptoed to the door and eased out before she spoke.

'Hey,' she said. 'How did it go?'

'Fine.' It was curt. 'You weren't there.'

'No.'

'Why not?' Kade asked.

'We…left early. It wasn't the right… We shouldn't have been there.'

'Why the hell not?'

She frowned. 'I'm sorry—have I upset you by not attending a ball that has nothing to do with me?'

'Is that why you left? Because you wanted it in your honour?'

'What—?' She exhaled. 'I do not have the energy for this. Let's talk in the morning.'

'You ran,' he said before she could move. The only reason she didn't move was because his voice was…raw. 'You ran away from that ball. I've never seen you run away from anything before.'

'I didn't run, I left. Because in the two hours I was there—*two hours*, Kade—not one person spoke with me. And we were drawing attention because we were clearly the only people who didn't know someone other than you and your parents in that room. While we're on that subject,' she continued, her tongue loose, 'why would you invite May to that ball? There were no children there. It put targets on our back when we already had them.'

'I didn't…' Kade trailed off, brow knitted. 'I didn't realise you would feel that way.'

'How could you not?' she asked softly, though her voice was strong. 'I thought there would be other children. I thought May would be…' She trailed off with a breath. 'I thought you'd want to protect her.'

When her knees suddenly felt weak, she sank down to the floor. Kade looked pained for a moment, but he joined her, back against the wall. They sat like that for a long time. There was no movement in the hall despite the many guests at the palace. For the first time, Amari wondered if that was because they'd been put in a different area from anyone else. Perhaps the other guests, the ones who weren't quite as common as them, got put in a fancier wing.

But even as she thought it, she felt shame. Nothing about the room or the way she'd been treated had made her feel common. Apart from the initial conversation she'd had with Kade's mother, a conversation she understood, she had never been made to feel like an outsider.

This evening had just…hit her harder than expected. And it had nothing to do with the event and everything to do with her feelings.

For Kade.

The ones she had convinced herself she did not have.

'I should have,' Kade said into the silence. 'I should have realised you would feel vulnerable.

I should have made more of an effort to be there with you.'

'No, you shouldn't have,' she argued. 'You're about to become *King*, Kade. You can't be my bodyguard.'

'Then what?' he asked. 'What could I have done to make this night easier for you?'

'I don't know,' she said a little helplessly. 'It would have helped if you'd told me May would be the only child there. I could have told you it was a bad idea then.'

'Would you still have come? Without her?'

'I… I don't know.'

He didn't reply for a while. 'Maybe I knew that. Maybe that's why I invited you both.'

'At her expense?' Amari asked, not quite believing what he'd said. 'You had her there, knowing it wasn't appropriate, because you wanted *me* there?'

'I… No.' He shook his head. 'No, that came out wrong.'

'How could it come out right?'

'I care about you,' he blurted out. She looked at him, her heart skipping when she saw the serious look in his eyes. 'I care about you both. I wanted you both there because…because it was important that you be there.'

He was being vague and they both knew it. But then he reached out and cupped her face. The heat was warm and soothing. It went straight to her heart, and it alarmed her. Because he had just revealed he hadn't been thinking about her kid. Or he had, but he hadn't thought about her enough to put his needs aside. He'd made a decision that worked for *him*.

Just like you've been doing.

No, she told that mental voice. It wasn't the same. It *wasn't*.

'I overreacted when I came here. I was upset. I thought...' He dropped his hand, but it fell to her lap and he left it there. 'When my mother made the announcement, the crowd wasn't surprised. It seemed they'd been expecting it these last weeks, especially with me taking more of a leading role in my mother's engagements.'

She wanted to hold his hand. To tangle their fingers together and let the warmth comfort her even more.

She didn't.

'There was applause and general approval, though I suppose that was because they're in my home and any other reaction would be frowned upon.' He paused. 'I didn't care. About any of it. I only cared that you weren't there. That at some point you had disappeared and I hadn't noticed. I worried, and eventually, my mother said something to me that snapped me out of it.'

'I'm sorry,' she breathed, because it was all she could manage. It felt like…like too much.

'I was being selfish,' he said when it became clear she wasn't going to reply. 'I should have thought about you not having anyone to talk to. I should have known May would be the only child there. But I only… I only thought about how much I wanted you both there for the most important moment of my life.'

She shifted away from him, forcing his hand to drop. Hurt flashed in his eyes, as if he knew she was trying to put distance between them.

'Kade—'

'Amari,' he interrupted. 'You can't tell me that you haven't at least thought about it.'

He didn't have to clarify for her to know that by 'it', he meant the two of them.

'What are you doing?' she whispered. 'We've talked about this. I'm not… We're not…'

'You are,' he said. 'We are.'

'No. No. We need to think about May,' she said a little desperately. 'Tonight was the perfect example of why this isn't good for her. She was clinging to my chest because people were staring at her, Kade. She was as quiet when I brought her back tonight as she was the night we first got here.'

'That shouldn't have happened,' he said in his

calm way. 'And it won't happen again. If you and I are together—'

She scrambled to stand, pacing so the energy in her body wouldn't turn into screaming.

'Amari,' Kade said, deliberately now. Somehow, he was standing, too. 'If you and I are together, no one will be allowed to make you or May feel that way again.'

'How can you be so sure?' she demanded. 'I've been a parent for *four* years and I haven't been able to guarantee anything for my daughter.' She fought against the burn at her eyes, in her throat. 'People say that when you become a parent, you only think about your child. But that's not really true. Your instinct to do what's best for you is still there. It happened tonight.'

'That's not fair. I didn't want—'

'I'm not talking about you,' she interrupted. 'I'm talking about me. I wanted to be there for you tonight. I wanted to see people's faces when they realised they were getting a damn good king. I should have realised…' her voice dropped to a whisper '…that this wouldn't be good for May. I should have asked whether she would be the only child there. But I didn't because I wanted to be there.'

She waited to catch her breath. Her emotions. When she had them in her hands—precariously, but still—she continued.

'That's what you make me do, Kade. You make me think about myself. About what I want. About…about you.'

'Because you want me.'

'Yes.' What was the point of denying it now? 'But wanting you made me move my child away from the only home she knows. It put her in a situation tonight that she shouldn't have been in.'

'I thought she was happy,' he pointed out quietly. 'Didn't you say being here was the best Christmas she's had?' She couldn't reply, but it didn't matter. He was talking again. 'She was quiet when she got here, but that didn't last. Neither will her discomfort at these events.'

'How do you know?'

'She has us.' The simple way he said it broke her heart. 'We'll be there for her. We'll protect her.'

'We won't.' She shook her head. 'We haven't.'

'We can't anticipate everything we need to protect her from. But we can learn. Now that we know better, we'll do better.'

'I know better,' Amari said with a firmness she didn't feel. 'This is not better.'

He studied her. 'You've already made up your mind, haven't you?'

She forced herself to nod.

Silence stretched before Kade took a step back. 'I'm sorry I bothered you.'

It was the disappointment in his tone that had

her blurting out, 'How can I be in a relationship with you and be a good mother to May?'

He paused, his eyes boring into hers in a way that made her feel as if he could see inside her. To that dark hole of feelings her words seemed to be coming from.

'If you wanted an answer,' he said slowly, 'I would have repeated your words to you. About how all anyone could ask for was someone to do their best for them. I believe you're doing that with May. I believe that, together, *we* could do that for May. But then, I believe that your happiness is as important as May's. There's nothing I can do if *you* don't believe that, Amari.' He let the silence linger before continuing. 'It's probably a good thing you don't want an answer, then.'

Seconds later, he was gone, leaving her feeling emptier than she had when she'd left the ballroom.

Kade avoided Amari the next day. He wasn't proud of it, but he kept hearing her words. *'How can I be in a relationship with you and be a good mother to May?'* If she truly believed that—and it was clear that she did—they couldn't be together. If the choice was between him and her child, he knew where he stood. Nowhere. And he couldn't blame her. Not when he understood her insecurities. Not when he knew how much she loved May. How she would do anything for her child. It broke his heart that she couldn't see she was a good mother. Or that she didn't believe she deserved love.

But how could he blame her when he loved May, too? One day without the kid and he already missed her. She was way too serious until she wasn't, and that combination had wormed its way deep into his heart. He hadn't only lost his chance with Amari; he'd lost his chance with May, too. And the double blow meant he needed time.

He hadn't expected them to leave while he took it.

'*What?*' he asked his mother. 'What do you mean they're gone?'

'I've already told you, Amari asked me to arrange for her and May to return to Swell Valley,' Winifred said, flicking out her wrists as she lay a napkin on her lap.

'And you did it?'

'You dealt with the situation quite well, Kade. The threat has passed.'

'How do you know that?'

'Pete says there hasn't been a single reporter around her home or store in the last week. Interest has died down, especially in light of last night's announcement.'

'That doesn't mean she's safe.'

'No,' his mother agreed. 'But she has state-of-the-art security systems now. We've also allocated guards to remain with her until they're sure no one is following her.' Her eyes flicked up. 'Additionally, I believe your lawsuit has made it clear pursuing her or May in any way will be dealt with severely. I think they've realised your private life is off limits. I suppose we'll see when you start dating again.'

'I won't—' He broke off. Curled his hand into a fist. 'Why didn't you tell me?'

'You would have spent the time trying to convince me they should stay.' Winifred picked up her coffee, took a sip before continuing. 'We've made too many decisions for them, Kade. The least we could do was respect this one.'

Kade stared at the space across from him. Amari used to sit there. May would sometimes sit next to her, sometimes next to him. The fact that they weren't there now made him feel empty. The table felt too big, his chest too hollow. His mind couldn't fully process that they were gone.

But his mother was right. He had realised that the night before, when Amari told him about what happened at the ball. *He* had decided he wanted them there. Both of them. He hadn't thought about how it would be for them. He hadn't even spoken with Amari about it. After the last time he'd made a decision for her, he'd thought he'd learnt his lesson. But apparently he hadn't, and it killed him.

It was why he hadn't proposed. He had made that decision all by himself, too, without talking to her about it. Without taking her feelings into account. His love for her didn't change that marriage would change her life. Everything she knew would be different. Even if she loved him, too—and he wasn't sure that was the extent of her feelings for him—she needed to have agency in this decision. He wouldn't put her in the situation where she had to decide something this important until he could prepare her for it.

Maybe he had learnt his lesson. It was a pity it was too late.

'I thought you were planning to propose, son,' his father said.

Kade's head lifted. 'How could you possibly know that?'

'We know everything,' his mother said breezily. 'What happened?'

Trying to figure out how he felt about his parents' knowledge of his life took too much energy. He sighed. 'It would be selfish to ask her to marry me. I couldn't do that to her again.'

'What do you mean?'

'I wanted her at the ball for me. I didn't think about how vulnerable it would make her feel, knowing only us. I didn't even consider whether it would be appropriate for May to attend when she would be the only child there.'

His mother glanced at Deacon. 'We should have thought about that. We could have invited some of Amari's friends from home. Maybe we could have planned a mini ball for the children.'

'You would have done that?' Kade asked.

Winifred gave him a shrewd look. 'You know we're fond of Amari and May. The last thing we wanted was to make them feel out of place when we very much want their place to be in this family.'

He blinked. 'Your support here is making me feel rather strange.'

'You're being foolish,' Winifred said. 'We knew you wanted to marry Amari and we didn't interfere. That must have told you how we feel.'

It took him a moment. 'I tend to need to hear these things.'

Winifred rolled her eyes. 'Tell me you at least told her what she needs to hear, then.'

He stared.

'That you love her, son,' Deacon said.

'Oh. I... No.'

'Why not?'

'I was worried—'

He exhaled. He wasn't sure he wanted to re-hash his love life with his parents. But as he looked at them, he saw nothing but love. Well, he saw impatience and curiosity, too, but he knew it was because they loved him. And for the first time in his life, he realised he was loved unconditionally.

All his worries about his mother's expectations of him, all his fears of disappointing her, had blinded him to the fact that she loved him. Both his parents did. And they supported him.

Who might he have been if he'd spent his energy claiming that instead of his anxieties?

He would never know. But realising he was loved unconditionally made him realise he loved unconditionally, too. And if he didn't tell Amari that, she'd spend her energy on the bad instead of the good, too. He needed to give her a chance to claim the good. He owed it to the both of them.

'I have to go,' he said, pushing out from the table.

He didn't miss his parents' smiles of approval as he left the room.

CHAPTER EIGHTEEN

It was Christmas Eve and Amari was staring at her empty store.

She hadn't been back since she'd got back home from Daria. Pete had been waiting for her when she'd got to her house. When she'd told him her plans to leave the store closed until after Christmas, he'd offered to run things until Christmas Eve. It was only for two days, so she'd accepted. Except she hadn't been accepting because it was only for two days. She'd been accepting because she was a coward who couldn't bear to be in a space she had once shared with the man she loved.

That realisation had hit her the moment her flight from Daria had taken off. The impact was nowhere as severe as she expected. It told her that her heart had been ahead of her brain for a long time.

But it didn't matter. She had chosen to come home and figure out how to be a better parent to May. It didn't matter that every time she thought about it, she heard Kade telling her she was already doing her best. And that she deserved to be happy. That May deserved to see her happy.

And now she was standing in her store on Christmas Eve, trying to figure out whether running the place still made her happy.

'The last two days I've spent at home have been really great,' she said out loud. 'I got to spend time prepping the house for Christmas with May. She loved it, though we did have to work through her feelings about leaving Daria. She wasn't thrilled that she didn't even get to say goodbye to Kade.'

Neither had Amari, but that was for the best.

'But the last two weeks without you has been... eye-opening. It's not you, I don't think. It was more spending time with May. And finding out I really like working with kids who aren't my own. Who would have thought it?' She ran a hand over the shelf in front of her. 'I need to figure out how to balance you with those other things. And I don't know how to do that right now.'

She would have spent longer thinking about it if the bell to the door hadn't rung. She whirled around. Her heart just about stopped.

'Kade.' It came out like some kind of breathy prayer. She cleared her throat. 'Wh-what are you doing here?'

'I don't have a job any more?'

He said the words with his unbearable charm.

Oh, she'd missed him. And the thought of it made her want to throw something at him. The thought, and the fact that he was standing in front of her looking so damn handsome in his perfect suit that fitted his perfect body. She could still feel it beneath her fingers.

'You have more important jobs.'

'I love you.'

She stared at him. 'What. The. *Hell?*'

'I didn't get to tell you that before you left.'

'That's why I didn't say goodbye, genius. So you didn't get *to* say it.'

His brow furrowed. 'You knew?'

'No. Not for sure.' She closed her eyes. Maybe it would help silence the echo of his *I love you* in her head. It didn't. She looked at him. 'It doesn't change anything.'

'It does.' He took a small step forward. 'Now you know for sure. And you can make a decision.'

'Kade…' She shook her head. 'I told you that I don't know how to be a good mother to May and be in a relationship with you. That hasn't changed.'

'But you *are* a good mother.' His certainty had longing surging inside her. 'I don't know why you can't see it.'

'Because I do stupid things!' she exclaimed. 'I make mistakes that are selfish and I… I do things that my mother would do.'

'Do you?' he asked. 'When your father left, did your mother change her entire life so that you would have some semblance of family?'

Her lashes fluttered. 'No.'

'Did your mother ever think about your well-being when she took a job? Or when she was in a relationship?'

This time, she couldn't speak. She only shook her head.

'Did your mother berate herself because she didn't think she was doing enough for you? Did she always try to think of you? Did she think about your happiness before her own?'

Her eyes prickled, but she didn't realise she was crying until Kade brushed a thumb across her cheek.

'Those things are selfish, Amari,' he whispered. 'And you haven't done one of those things.'

'I… I…'

'Made mistakes, like we all do. But you do your best to learn from them. Even if you don't always succeed the next time, you try. Trying is the best you can do.'

She pursed her lips. 'Stop using my words against me.'

He chuckled, but the humour quickly faded. 'Wanting to be happy isn't selfish. Being happy isn't selfish. How can it be? You'll be showing May that thinking about other people *and* herself is okay. You'll be showing her that her feelings are every bit as important as anyone else's. You'll be showing her she deserves the life she wants.'

The stubborn side of her wanted to disagree. But she couldn't. She wanted May to have the best life she could possibly have. That meant thinking about her own needs. It meant valuing her happiness. How could she see that if Amari didn't show her?

It wouldn't be easy. She'd had too much practice branding every similarity she had with her mother as selfish. Yes, she made some mistakes, but the way she responded to them wasn't like her mother at all. It had taken Kade to outline the differences, even in those similarities. He could see them because he loved her. It terrified her.

'You seem pretty confident that what I want is you.'

'No.' He said it with a nervous laugh, though it sounded more like a simple burst of air. 'No, Amari.' He took a breath. 'I just… I love you. I love you exactly as you are. I'm not perfect. I will never be. And I'll make mistakes in our relationship and in my relationship with May. But I want to try. I want to be with you and raise May. I love her almost as much as I love you.'

She had never realised her heart wasn't whole until that point. Because now it felt whole. It felt full. He'd done that.

'I don't like your charm. I don't like that it utterly disarms me.'

His eyes widened. Slowly, the ends of his mouth followed.

'But I do like you. I like you exactly as you are. I like that you are a good man who sees the good in me. I like that you try, even when you don't think you are. I like that you can see me when I can't see myself.' She paused there because her throat got thick. 'I like it all so much that I... I might love you.'

He was grinning by the time she was done.

'Might?'

'Small steps.'

His smile somehow got bigger. She felt her own lips twitch.

'You love me,' he said.

She grunted.

'Maybe I need to say this to get you to admit it.' He suddenly got serious. 'I'll protect you. Both of you. As best I can.'

Her heart did the strange filling thing again. Strange because it was already full. Apparently, with him, her heart overflowed.

'I believe you. I trust you.'

'But do you love me?'

He was still trying to get her to say it when she kissed him.

EPILOGUE

One year later

AMARI COULDN'T BELIEVE that she was staring at her kingdom.

They were on the balcony of the palace, a part she hadn't seen when she'd visited the year before, looking out at all the people who had gathered to celebrate her marriage to Kade. A sea of faces she was now responsible for.

It didn't concern her nearly as much as it would have once upon a time. She had her husband by her side. She had her daughter by her side, too. She squeezed both their hands, clasped in hers as they, too, stared out at the crowd.

It hadn't been an easy transition to royal life. And it wasn't the transition *into* royal life that was the problem as much as transitioning *out of* the life she had built for her and May. She had sold the store, a heartbreaking decision that had had to be made. She had given up the lease on her home, said goodbye to her friends—her family—and asked them to visit. And she had tried to make May as comfortable as she could during the shift.

The year had been rough and long. Planning the wedding while finalising things in Swell Valley and learning about what her royal life would entail had seemed endless. But standing there, with their family together, happier than they had ever been, made it worth it. Especially when May had laughed more that day than Amari had heard in a year. It was all worth it.

'Ready?' Kade asked, turning to her.

She squeezed May's hand one last time before nodding at Queen Winifred. Her mother-in-law deftly distracted May, and Amari turned back to her King.

'Ready.'

Their lips touched in the sweetest kiss, though the heat wasn't far behind. It never was when they kissed these days. But today, there was promise in that heat. An acknowledgement that they would have a lifetime to sate it.

Amari smiled, her husband's mouth still against hers, her heart full.

* * * * *